Jessie groaned...

The sentry's head turned at once, and Jessie could tell that he'd seen her, for he took a step toward her. As he moved, he shifted the muzzle of the rifle to cover her. He bent forward as he peered through the darkness at her prone form.

"Who the hell are you?" he asked.

"Help me," Jessie moaned.

"Damned if you ain't a woman!" the sentry exclaimed as he bent still lower. "Who are you and what are you doing here?"

At that point Jessie struck...

— WESLEY ELLIS —

LONE STAR

AND THE LAND BARONS

J.®

A JOVE BOOK

LONE STAR AND THE LAND BARONS

A Jove Book/published by arrangement with
the author

PRINTING HISTORY
Jove edition/August 1986

ISBN: 0-515-08649-5

Chapter 1

Still half-asleep, Jessie stirred and moved to ease the cramp that was beginning to twitch in the calf of one leg. She'd been lying on her back when she woke up, and in turning to stretch the muscle that had begun aching, she felt her foot brush against warm, unfamiliar flesh.

Jessie snapped awake instantly. Her eyes opened in the darkness, and for a moment she thought she'd wakened in her own bedroom at the Circle Star. Out of habit she turned her head toward where the window that broke the wall of her bedroom would be. Instead of the familiar rectangle, only darkness met her eyes. Startled now, she started to sit up.

"Jessie?" a man's voice asked sleepily.

When Jessie heard the voice only inches from her ear, she recognized it at once. She relaxed as quickly as she had tensed a few seconds earlier.

"I'm sorry, Harmon," she said softly. "I didn't mean to disturb you, but for a minute I forgot where I was."

"Don't be sorry," Harmon Marsden told her. "I'm glad you woke up. We went to sleep far too early." The wailing of a locomotive's whistle drowned his words, and he stopped until the sound ended abruptly. "The train must've waked you," he said as the noise of the approaching locomotive grew louder. "That's the only disadvantage of trying to sleep in a private car on a railroad siding. There's always a train that passes on the next track and wakes you up. I ought to be used to it by now, but I'm not."

"Don't worry," Jessie said. "The train won't bother us long. They don't stop at this little place unless they're flagged or there's a passenger wanting to get off in order to go on to the Circle Star or one of the other ranches."

They lay silently as the rumbling sounds of the train grew louder. Another whistle sounded so loud that the engine seemed to be in the private car with them. Then the rails began clicking as the locomotive passed them.

"This one's stopping," Marsden commented as the harsh grind of its brakes filled the air.

"One of my neighbors must be getting back from a trip," Jessie said. "The train won't stay long."

Almost before she'd stopped speaking, the whistle tooted two sharp blasts, and the huffing of the engine began anew. The clicking and grinding of wheels on the tracks sounded again, but faded quickly, and soon the night outside was quiet once more.

"We won't be disturbed again tonight," Jessie said as she snuggled closer to her lover. "And while I'm thinking of it, you greeted me so enthusiastically that I never did get a chance to tell you how glad I am that you had time to stop here. It's been a long time since we were able to be together."

"Too long," he replied, "and I wasn't sure you'd even be at the Circle Star when I sent that telegram asking you to meet me. Ever since I got your answer, all I've been able to think about is seeing you again. I'm glad you were at the ranch to get my message."

"Oh, I've settled down there until the men get through cutting the cattle into winter herds and driving them to where they'll be grazing for the next few months," Jessie said. "This is the first time in two or three years that I've been able to be at the Circle Star while the hands are working steers."

One of Marsden's hands was brushing across Jessie's hip as she spoke, and she lay quietly while his fingertips caressed a warm trail over her soft skin until they reached her breasts. When Marsden touched her rosettes and they began budding under his gentle tweaking, she lay back, revelling in the sensations that were beginning to stir in response to her lover's caresses.

After a moment she turned on her side and her lips sought his. They kissed, tongues entwining, and held the kiss until both of them were breathless. When they parted, gasping, Jessie fell back on her pillow. Marsden dropped his head to find her budded tips with his mouth, and Jessie lay quietly while he soothed each of them with his lips and tongue before trailing kisses down her soft, warm skin.

Jessie parted her thighs to let Marsden's head slip between them. She shivered as her lover's tongue began a lingering exploration of their satiny inner skin. Then she felt the moisture of his lips and the gentle rasping of his tongue as he probed for the firm button that dwelt within. When he found it, she gasped softly as he settled down to laving it with his tongue's agile tip.

Closing her eyes, Jessie spread her thighs wider while Marsden continued his undulating caresses. For a while she controlled her own response, but as her lover's attentions continued she let the waves of sensation that had begun flowing through her body mount of their own accord until he'd brought her to the point where she could no longer wait.

"Come into me now," she said, her voice soft and urgent. "Hurry! Take me before the storm you're raising bursts!"

Marsden slid between Jessie's sprawled thighs while she groped for his bulging shaft, found it, guided it, and gasped with delight as he lunged home. Locking her legs around his hips, Jessie pulled herself up until Marsden was fully buried and then responded to his lusty thrusts by raising her hips with a twisting motion each time he stroked.

Jessie had already been aroused by the attention her lover had lavished on her before going into her. She felt herself mounting to a climax too quickly and called on her knowledge of the sexual arts. She kept her mind in control of her body and held herself poised on the brink of total response to Marsden's rhythmic stroking while he continued to thrust with increasing vigor until she could feel his body start trembling.

Only when his strokes speeded to a trip hammer pace and he began quivering at the ragged edge of his climax did Jessie release herself. Marsden thrust deeply into her as he groaned and cried out, and Jessie's throbbing sighs of satisfaction mingled with his. They gasped and shuddered together, their cries breaking the quiet of the private car as they passed through their final climactic moments. The last frenzy of their threshing faded and stopped. They lay panting, their breathing ragged, their bodies limp and spent.

Totally relaxed and with the body of her lover weighting her with pleasant warmth, Jessie was almost at the point of dozing again when Harmon spoke.

"I still think we ought to get married, Jessie," he half-whispered. "Isn't there a chance at all that you'll change your mind about me?"

4

"You're always somewhere in my mind," she said. "I never forget you, even though we can't be together as often as we might choose to be if both of us were free."

"That's not what I mean, Jessie," Harmon replied.

"I know," she told him, "you're thinking about us getting married. But I also know that what you and I might want isn't always possible for us to get."

"You're saying that we're both prisoners of our fathers?" There was perplexity in Marsden's voice. He shifted his weight off Jessie and stretched out beside her on the wide, soft bed that took up most of the space in the room that had been formed by partitioning one end of his private railroad coach.

"I don't think of myself as a prisoner," Jessie replied. The frown that had formed on her face was invisible in the darkness, but it was reflected in her voice.

"I think of myself that way sometimes," he confessed. "I know it's not fair because father worked hard to get all the things he passed on to me in his will."

Harmon Marsden's father had been an industrial tycoon and had left his fortune to his son, just as Alex Starbuck had bequeathed his enormous wealth to Jessie, his daughter. She'd met Marsden several years earlier—a chance encounter in the office of the president of a bank in which both fathers had owned blocks of stock. Jessie and Harmon had been attracted to each other at that first meeting. They'd become lovers in spite of the separation imposed on them by the responsibilities they had inherited. Since their first meeting, they'd been able to be together only six times, either during Jessie's rare trips to the East or during his trips across the continent when he could arrange his schedule to stop in Texas.

Jessie said, "I'm sorry you feel chained, but I'm glad that I don't. I know how important the responsibilities Alex carried were to him, and I wouldn't feel comfortable if I

5

didn't do all that I could to carry them out."

Jessie could speak no more plainly, for among her inheritances from Alex was the effort he'd been making to crush an insidious and vicious European cartel. The cartel was a group of European noblemen and top industrial leaders who were working with single-minded and totally unscrupulous intensity to gain control of the wealth and industrial might of the United States, its aim being to make America subservient to them. Killers hired by the cartel had murdered Alex some years earlier in a surprise attack against the Circle Star.

"I could help you, Jessie," Marsden said, "just as you could help me."

Forgetting that he could not see her in the darkness, Jessie shook her head. "I'm sorry," she said. "There's a part of me that would love to be with you all the time, but there's another part that tells me it just wouldn't work out for either of us."

"Together we could do a great deal more than either of us can do alone," he suggested.

Jessie decided that it was time to end their discussion before it became an argument. She said, "All we're sure of right now is that there's one thing we enjoy doing together. Why don't we just limit ourselves to that for the moment? After all, it may be a long time before we can be together again."

As she spoke, Jessie slid one hand gently down his body until it reached his crotch and closed it over his flaccid shaft.

"I won't argue with you now, Jessie," he said. "Being together occasionally is better than not seeing each other at all. But don't expect me to give up."

"I won't," she said as her hand began squeezing him in a gentle, rhythmic pulsing as a preliminary to bringing him erect again. "I wouldn't want you to. You must know how much I enjoy being with you."

"Then just think what it would be like if we—" he began to say.

Jessie cut off his words by closing his lips with hers, and then the two were silent except for whispered endearments as they moved once more into the world of shared pleasure that requires no words.

"When will you be going East again?" Harmon asked Jessie as she stood up, now fully dressed.

Only a few moments ago when she'd slid quietly out of bed, the interior of the car had been dark. Now she could see Harmon as he rose from the bed and took a dressing gown off the wall hook close by. As Jessie rose from the chair where she'd been sitting and pulling on her boots, she saw the growing light of dawn between the edges of the drawn shades and the window frames.

"I don't know," she replied, stamping her feet to get them settled snugly into her boots. "But aren't you going to stop on your way back home?"

He shook his head. "I've got to go back by way of Chicago and Pittsburgh. Carnegie's creating a lot of trouble in the steel industry, and a few of us have agreed to try to calm things down."

"It's not going to create a panic, is it?" Jessie frowned. "I remember how busy Alex was during the one that took the country a few years ago."

"We're going to try to stop another one before it starts," he replied. "But don't be surprised if you get a wire from me asking for you to throw the weight of the Starbuck interests on our side."

"You'll get my support, of course," Jessie said quickly, sliding her arms into the well-worn leather vest that she usually favored when on the range. "But I don't want to go East unless there's a real crisis. I've spent so little time lately on the Circle Star that I want to stay here as long as I can."

"I wish you'd stay right here longer," Marsden said, taking her in his arms. "It'll be almost an hour before the train will pick up this car."

Jessie shook her head. "I've got to be back at the ranch before the men start out, and I should've left before now."

She raised her lips for a clinging good-bye kiss, then went down the car's steps, and made a final jump to the ground. After turning to wave good-bye, Jessie started for the small corral where Sun was waiting. The great golden palomino neighed a welcome as she approached, and she ran her hand down the magnificent stallion's head and caressed Sun's velvety nose for a moment before saddling him.

As she rode away from the corral, she turned for a final look. Harmon was standing in his dressing gown in the vestibule of his railroad coach, and when he saw her turning to look back, he waved. Jessie waved her farewell, then dug her heels into Sun's flanks, and let the golden horse set its own pace as it carried her through the soft dawn that was beginning to reveal the expanse of prairie that surrounded her.

Marsden's last remarks about the possibility of new troubles in the steel industry were still in Jessie's mind as she rode. She wondered if the ruthless cartel that Alex had battled for so many years was establishing a new front in its unceasing effort to get control of America's industrial might.

Jessie had not really understood the cartel's threat until she'd found herself in control of Alex's vast holdings after his murder. Like so many self-made men, her father had preferred to fight his battle alone. It was typical of him, she thought.

Starting as a young man with a small Oriental imports

store in San Francisco, Alex had worked so diligently that when a battered freighter had been offered for sale he'd accumulated enough capital to buy it. Carrying his own goods from the Orient had improved sales in the store so greatly that he'd soon been able to buy a second vessel and to lay the foundation for his own shipping line.

When iron hulls began to replace wooden ones in shipbuilding, Alex had been astute enough to see the future trend and had acquired a small mill. From that point his reputation for honest dealing and diligence had spread. He became a major importer of Oriental wares and expanded his merchant fleet. The mill led to his establishing a foundry. Then the foundry created a need for iron ore, and Alex bought mines and set up a smelter.

Before he'd entered his thirties, the close-knit San Francisco banking community had accepted him, and he'd added a financial base to his holdings by buying bank stocks. Brokerage and real estate operations had followed, giving him a hold in the key financial circles of the East. The Starbuck interests grew to take in copper and silver mines, timberlands, and great tracts of farmland in California's fertile river valleys.

Early in his meteoric career, young Starbuck's abilities had drawn the attention of a cartel formed by European industrialists and nobility. The cartel was a two-headed organization. Its visible head was devoted to industry and finance, but its hidden head carried a single idea: to grasp control of America's burgeoning resources and then to dominate the world.

Invited to join the cartel, Alex investigated it before responding. When he discovered its true intention, his patriotic spirit was outraged. He declared war on the cartel and set out to thwart its sinister aims. Because its influence was so widespread, Alex had been forced to move with caution. For the most part, he'd carried on a largely solitary battle, his only allies being the few men in key positions in his own industrial empire whom he knew he could trust fully.

Even Jessie had not at first understood Alex's full commitment to his efforts to save the America he loved. Then, going over Alex's papers and aided by Ki, who had been Alex's strong right hand and was now hers, she learned of the sinister plot and began to grasp its full implications. Not only to carry on the fight that Alex had begun, but also to protect the land that she loved, she resolved to carry on his fight.

Now, riding back to the Circle Star, the sprawling Texas ranch that Alex had created and that she had come to love as much as he had, Jessie breathed the cool air of the Texas prairie and watched the rim of the sun beginning its slow rise above the horizon.

"Let's have a gallop, Sun," Jessie called to the big palomino. "I know you've got kinks in your legs, but I need to feel the wind on my face! Go, now!"

Sun responded to Jessie's voice as much as he did to the nudge of her boot. He snorted and gave a mighty surge to his powerful legs, and Jessie bent forward in her saddle as the short grass on each side of her blurred when the palomino responded to her urging.

A few hundred yards ahead of them the trail to the Circle Star's ranch house slanted up a low rise in the generally level land and disappeared below the ridge's crest. Sun reached his full stride a few moments before they topped the rise, and Jessie braced herself for the surge of added speed that she knew the big stallion would put on as he started down the grade.

Sun saw the huddled figure lying beside the trail an instant before Jessie did. He swerved to the opposite side of the trail, and Jessie swayed in her saddle at his unexpected move. Then she, too, saw the man lying beside the trail.

She tugged lightly on the reins. Sun slowed and then stopped. His speed had carried them well beyond the still form. Jessie twitched the reins, and Sun wheeled. At a walk now, he returned to the motionless man who lay on the ground beside the trail.

Jessie scanned the prairie in all directions during the few moments required for Sun to close the distance between the spot where he'd stopped and the man. Even though the man did not move, she drew her Colt as the palomino drew closer. Then as the man showed no sign of consciousness, she reined in and dismounted.

At close range now, she could see the blood on the back of the man's coat as well as the butt of a holstered revolver under the coat's rumpled fabric. She stopped beside the still figure and glanced quickly around the prairie. There was no sign of movement, and Jessie dropped to one knee beside the recumbent form.

Only now could she see the slow swelling and contracting of the man's ribs that told her he was still breathing. She glanced at the blood that spread in a huge blot on the back of his jacket and then grasped his extended arm with both hands and carefully turned him over.

"Don Carter!" she gasped when she saw his face. "But what would he be doing here at the Circle Star?"

To her surprise, Carter opened his eyes. His eyelids fluttered for a moment and then his eyes focused on Jessie's face.

"Miss Jessie!" he whispered, his voice weak and strained. "I was hoping I'd get to you in time, but it looks like they caught up with me. You—" He gasped for breath and uttered a moaning sob. Then his eyes closed again and he lay silent.

11

★

Chapter 2

For a moment, Jessie thought that Carter was dead. Then she saw that his chest was still rising and falling slowly. Pushing aside her question about why he was here, Jessie lowered his limp form to the ground and whistled for Sun to come to her.

Trained to obey, the golden stallion moved to where Jessie kneeled beside Carter and then stood motionless. Jessie slid her hands into the unconscious man's armpits, and using every bit of her considerable strength, she lifted the unconscious Carter to his feet and supported his sagging body while she staggered the short step necessary to reach Sun's side. After two efforts failed, she managed to get his arms draped over Sun's withers.

With Carter's limp weight partly supported by Sun's sturdy back, it was relatively easy to slide the wounded man's unresisting form forward until it was draped across the palomino's back in front of the saddle.

While she caught her breath after completely lifting

Carter, Jessie glanced at the trail and the ground on each side of it, searching for a clue of some kind that would tell her what had taken place. The trail showed many hoofprints, but they were so mixed up on the baked ground that even her skilled eyes could not find a pattern that had any meaning. Swinging onto Sun's back again, she nudged his flank with the toe of her boot, and the big horse started moving along the trail at a steady walk.

Not daring to risk a faster pace, Jessie kept the palomino at a walk all the way to the Circle Star headquarters. Now she had time to wonder why Carter had returned to the Circle Star after having resigned his job as foreman more than two years ago to establish his own spread in the Wyoming Territory. Puzzling over the question had brought no answer by the time the big stone ranch house was in sight.

By now the sun had climbed high into the sky. Carter had not stirred during the agonizingly slow ride. His breathing had been labored and shallow. He remained unconscious. As Jessie rounded the corner of the main house, Ki came out of the front door. He saw the limp form draped over Sun and began running toward Jessie.

"Trouble?" he asked. "Are you all right?"

"I'm fine," Jessie assured Ki as he took Sun's bridle and started leading the horse the short distance to the door.

Ki nodded. There were no secrets between them, though the two were not in the habit of discussing their private lives with each other. Ki had been Alex Starbuck's top hand for many years and, after Alex's murder, had stayed with Jessie, not only helping her to recover from the shock of her father's death, but also filling her in on the details of business transactions that had not been completed before Alex's murder.

Ki was the son of a Japanese mother whose family was one of the oldest and richest in Japan and the American husband she'd married in defiance of her family's wishes. Her culture did not accept such marriages, and due to his mixed blood, Ki had inherited his mother's estrangement when both she and his father met untimely deaths.

Embittered by the wall that his grandparents had raised between themselves and his mother after her marriage, Ki sought the only occupation open to a youth of his noble birth, that of a roaming warrior. In Okinawa, where the art of hands-only combat had been evolving for more than a hundred years, Ki moved from one master teacher to another until his skills had been finely honed. Then he traveled restlessly until by chance he met Alex Starbuck, who had been a friend of his dead parents.

Alex had hired Ki as an assistant and had come to look on him as a son. During the years Ki had spent with Alex, he'd learned much about the Starbuck industrial empire and now served Jessie in the same capacity he'd served Alex.

"How about him?" Ki asked, inclining his head to indicate the limp form of Carter, who still hung across Sun's withers. "Is he alive or dead? And who is he?"

"He's alive," Jessie replied. "And he's Don Carter."

"You mean the same Don Carter who used to be foreman here?" Ki frowned. "What happened, Jessie?"

"He's the Don Carter we know, all right," Jessie told Ki as she swung out of her saddle. "And I'm as curious as you are to know what happened. He's been unconscious since I found him lying on the trail a few miles from the railroad, and I haven't any idea at all what he's doing here or how he got wounded."

"How long ago did you find him?"

Glancing at the sun, Jessie replied, "More than two hours, closer to three. Now, let's get him inside and see if we can bring him to."

"Hadn't we better take him to the little bunkhouse?" Ki

suggested. "It's right by the cookhouse where it'll be easy for Gimpy to take care of him."

"Don didn't start here to see Gimpy, Ki," Jessie said. "I'm sure he has something important to tell me, or he wouldn't have left the Wyoming Territory, busy as he must be on his spread. I want him to be in the house where I can get to him right away when he comes to."

"You're right, of course." Ki nodded. "As soon as we've carried him upstairs, I'll go get Gimpy to come and take a look at him, though."

With Ki supporting the unconscious man on one side and Jessie on the other, they made a quick job of getting him upstairs and into bed. While Ki went to get the cook, Jessie slipped Carter's coat off and was unbuttoning his shirt when Ki returned with Gimpy limping behind him and carrying a flour sack.

"What's all this Ki was telling me about Don Carter being shot, Jessie?" the gnarled, old cook asked as he came in. "Who'd wanta be shooting a good man like him?"

"That's what I asked myself while I was bringing him home," Jessie replied. "Help me get his shirt off and we'll see how badly hurt he is."

Gimpy joined Jessie beside the bed and lifted Carter's torso while she stripped off his shirt. "Looks to me like he was shot from behind," Gimpy said as he looked at Carter's muscular chest. "That there's a bullet wound up by his right nipple, if you'll excuse me talking plain. It's a fresh one, only about halfways healed up, but it ain't bleeding none. Let's take a look at his back."

Jessie took a close look at the barely healed scar, a fingertip-size, puckered red dot, on Charter's chest while she and Ki and Gimpy were turning him.

"You're right, Gimpy," she said. "It's a bullet wound and not a very old one, either. But he wasn't shot on his way to the ranch."

16

"Now, this hole here where the bullet came out, it's all busted open," Gimpy said. He bent down to examine the wound at the edge of Carter's shoulder and then took a wide roll of linen bandage from his flour sack. "I'll fix him up in no time so he won't bleed no more."

After tearing off a short length of bandage from his roll, the old cook folded the cloth into a neat square and placed it over the old bullet wound. Ki stepped to the bed and lifted Carter's torso while Gimpy wound two or three turns of the bandage to hold the pad in place. His gnarled fingers moving with surprising deftness. He slid the end of the bandage under one of the layers that encircled Carter's chest and tied it.

"Now, that's all he really needs," he told Jessie and Ki. "Along with some good grub and a little rest."

"Thank you, Gimpy," Jessie said. "I'm glad you decided to stop wandering and stay here at the Circle Star. You're as good as a doctor."

"Well, I seen enough doctoring while I was rambling to pick up a bit," Gimpy told her, putting his roll of bandage back in the flour sack. "Now, just keep Don quiet for a day or two, and he'll be good as new." Gimpy had started limping out of the room, but he stopped at the door and turned back. "You can be real sure it wasn't no fresh wound, Ki. I got an idea Don jest run outa patience and took off his bandage afore that hole in his back was healed up good, and he done too much moving around. Maybe he got throwed by a strange hoss. You told me Jessie said he was heading here from the railroad."

"Yes, he was," Jessie said, "but there wasn't any sign of a horse where I found him."

"If it was one of those half-wild broncos the station agent rents, it'd have bolted and might be still running," Ki said. "But I'd say Gimpy's figured out what happened."

"Well, that makes me feel better," Jessie said. "If Don's

just suffering from loss of blood, all that we need to do is to keep him quiet and feed him well for a week or so."

"I'll see he's fed," Gimpy said. "Don was real good to me when I first came here. I figure I owe him nigh as much as I do you and Ki. Now, you don't need me around here no more, so I better get back to my kitchen."

After the cook left, Jessie told Ki, "Don must certainly have something important on his mind to make a trip all the way back here from Wyoming."

"It's important, all right, Jessie," Carter said, his voice hoarse and a bit uncertain.

Jessie and Ki turned to face the bed. Carter had risen to prop himself up on one elbow. His brows were drawn together in a worried frown.

"How do you feel?" Jessie asked.

"A little bit shaky, but I'll get along fine," he said. "I need to talk to you right away, Jessie. That's what I come all the way down here from Wyoming to do. If I—"

"Hush, Don," Jessie told him firmly. "Whatever's on your mind isn't so important that it can't wait until you've gotten your strength back." She turned to Ki. "You might tell Gimpy that Don's come to and ask him to bring him something to eat. And while he's at it, I could do with a bite of breakfast and some hot coffee myself."

"If I know Gimpy, he's got your breakfast and Don's just about ready to serve by now," Ki replied. "All I'll need to do is tell him you're ready to eat."

After Ki left, Jessie turned back to Carter and said, "I don't want you to try to talk too much, Don, but I know you wouldn't have come all this distance unless you had something important on your mind. Does it have anything to do with that bullet wound you're carrying?"

Carter told her, his hand going instinctively to the bandage that circled his chest, "I got it close to a month ago."

"You were in a gunfight?"

18

Carter shook his head. "You know me better than that, Jessie. Gunfighting ain't my style. Some bushwhacker that I never did even see come to my spread and tried to kill me."

"And you don't know why?"

"I can't prove why," he replied. "But I know, all right, or at least I think I do. That's what I've come down here to talk to you about."

Before Carter could go on, Ki and Gimpy returned. Ki was balancing a plate in each hand while the cook carried a coffeepot and cups. After arranging Carter in bed so that he could eat and getting Jessie settled with her breakfast at the small bedside table, Gimpy left. Ki pulled up a chair and sat down between Jessie and Carter, who were both eating hungrily. He sat quietly, waiting for them to finish breakfast. At last Jessie pushed aside her empty plate and refilled her cup.

"From what you've said, Don, there's trouble brewing for you on that spread you've started," she said. "I know you well enough—and so does Ki—to realize you're not causing it. But who is?"

Carter did not reply for a moment, but then he said, "I'm not really sure, Jessie."

"What kind of trouble?" Ki asked. "It surely didn't start when somebody put that bullet through you."

"Oh, no," Carter said. "And there wasn't any kind of trouble the first year I was up there. I got my house built and put up a little stable. So far I've just got a couple of hands working for me. I don't need anything big like the Circle Star."

Seeing that Carter was having trouble trying to find a starting point, Jessie said, "Suppose you go back to the beginning, Don. I don't know much about the Wyoming Territory, and I'm not sure that Ki does, either. All we're sure of is that when you left the Circle Star you went up

19

there and bought some land to start your own spread."

"Well, the best land I could find by the time I got up there was above the North Platte," Carter said, frowning. "I looked around down to the south, but the Englishmen who've been moving into Colorado had already bought up grazing rights to most of the good range to the south."

"You'd be up on the land east of the Bighorn Mountains, then?" Jessie asked.

Carter nodded. "That's right. It's what the Wyoming folks call Powder River country, Jessie. Pretty much like the range farther south in Colorado, except there's not as much water on it. You know what everybody says about the Powder River, I guess."

Jessie smiled. "A mile wide and a foot deep. At least, that's what I've heard."

"It's pretty much right, too," Carter said. "But there's a few little creeks that run into the Powder or flow south into the North Platte."

"I've seen a little of that country," Ki said. He turned to Jessie and said, "When Alex first started thinking about a ranch where he wouldn't have a lot of close neighbors, he looked around in Wyoming Territory a little bit. I went with him, of course, so I remember something about it."

"Well, it was the best land I saw that I could file on, and I could afford to buy enough to give me the range to run the size spread I want," Carter said. "There was plenty of open range all around where I picked out, but the Englishmen had already driven up the price so high a man like me couldn't afford to buy much of it."

"And now you say they're beginning to move more completely into Wyoming?" Jessie asked.

"They begun buying a little bit before I got my place picked out," Carter nodded. "But mostly they was interested in land that was closer to Colorado, and they had

20

about all the good range in the south part of the territory all tied up."

"And now they're moving north?" she inquired.

"That's the way it looks to me," Carter replied. "Except they're not buying outright. They're taking out options, and if they don't decide to buy in two or three years, all they'll be out of pocket is their down payment. But you know I don't have anything like as much as them lords and earls and counts can come up with, Jessie."

"Do you need some help, Don?" Jessie asked. "Because if you do, I'll be glad to—"

"Now, hold on!" Carter broke in. "I didn't come here to beg you for a handout, Jessie. I thank you for offering, but I wouldn't feel right about it—now that I don't work for you any longer."

"You're welcome to it if you need it," she told him. "And it wouldn't be a handout. I'd advance you what you need for the down payment on the land you want, but I'll hold a first mortgage on it until you've paid off your loan. It'd be a straight business deal, not charity."

"You sure make it sound good," Carter replied. "But I'd still rather not feel beholden. No, the reason I came here to talk to you, Jessie, is because I remember that one time I heard Alex talking about a bunch of them people from Europe who was buying things up, land and factories and banks and mines and all like that. It wasn't any of my affair, but I could tell he was upset about it, so it sorta stuck in my mind."

Jessie kept surprise from showing in her voice when she asked Carter, "Do you think that's what's happening in the Wyoming Territory, Don?"

"I don't know as I can answer that, Jessie," Carter said, a thoughtful frown on his face. "But I was serious about wanting that land down to the south of my place, so I took the time to go into Laramie and ask about borrowing some money from them so I'd have something to dicker with if I decided to try for a deal on it."

"And they turned you down?"

"Well, they didn't say yes and they didn't say no, but the way they talked seemed sorta funny. They told me this Englishman had been in talking to them about the same thing."

"And they'd promised him a loan?" Ki asked when Carter paused.

"They didn't come right out and say so. It wasn't so much what they said to me as it was the way they talked." He looked from Ki to Jessie and asked, "Am I making sense, Jessie? Can you come up with a reason my money didn't seem as good as some English lord's?"

"Do you remember the Englishman's name?" Jessie asked.

"It was either Harrington or Herrington. I didn't catch it exactly because that fellow I was talking to only said it one time. After that all he said was his lordship. But it was the way that fellow in the bank acted that got me suspicious, Jessie. Once he got started telling me about that Englishman, it seemed to me like he was afraid to talk to me."

"And that reminded you of what Alex had said?"

"It didn't until after somebody bushwhacked me. I had time to think about things while that bullet hole was healing up."

"You figure that is the only reason somebody would want to put a bullet through you?" she asked.

"As far as I know, Jessie, I ain't got an enemy in the world. I guess there are a lot of cowhands who might be mad at me. I've had to run a few shiftless ones and careless ones off my place up in Wyoming, but there sure aren't any killers among 'em."

Jessie nodded. "It does hang together when you put it that way," she said.

"That's the way I figure it." Carter nodded. "And I owe Alex a lot, Jessie. I figure that since you're sorta standing in his boots now, you want to know about what's going on, provided something is going on up there."

"I'll tell you what, Don," Jessie said, "you've had a pretty bad time since last night. Suppose you think hard about everything you've run into up in Wyoming that's made you suspicious. Rest while you're thinking, and we'll talk about this later."

★

Chapter 3

"Do you really think the cartel's trying to get hold of the cattle ranges up in the Wyoming Territory?" Ki asked Jessie as they walked downstairs.

"Nothing that bunch of crooks does would surprise me," Jessie answered. "How many times have we seen this kind of pattern shaping up before—when the cartel stretches its claws for a grab, Ki?"

"So many that I've lost track," Ki replied, following Jessie down the hall. "And Don Carter's not the kind of man who'd do a lot of wild talking."

"Or wild dreaming, either," Jessie said. "He's not long on imagination, but I'd give him a high score for memory, the way he remembered what he'd heard and seen when he was with Alex. And I guess he gets good marks for deduction, the way he put all those small signs together and came down here to tell us about them, knowing we'd be interested."

By now Jessie and Ki were in the room that Alex used as his study. It was a big room, dominated by a massive fieldstone fireplace that took up almost the entire wall at one end and the large portrait of Jessie's dead mother at the opposite end. Against the back wall between two windows stood the well-worn oaken desk that Alex had bought when he started his first business venture in San Francisco.

In the room were a large divan and several chairs, upholstered in leather that years of use and careful attention had polished satiny smooth. The chairs still retained a faint fragrance of Alex's aromatic pipe tobacco. In Jessie's memory of her childhood days when Alex would clasp her in his big work-scarred hands and hold her high above his head, the scent of that tobacco was always flowing from her father's pipe, and even now when she snuggled into one of the chairs, the aroma of pipe tobacco that lingered faintly in the leather evoked memories of Alex.

This time, Jessie did not go to one of the chairs when she and Ki entered the study. Instead, she stopped just inside the door at a tall oak cabinet. The doors that closed off its two bottom shelves were always left unlocked while she was at the Circle Star, and she opened them, looked for a moment, then took out a book, and carried it to the desk.

Opening it, she leafed through pages until she'd found the one she'd been looking for. A sheet of folded paper lay on the page that she was bending over. Jessie picked it up and gestured for Ki to join her. He glanced at the page and saw that Jessie had opened the book to a large-scale map of the Wyoming Territory.

"Of course," he said. "The state maps Alex commissioned when he first began to expand the Starbuck enterprises. I'd almost forgotten about them; we use them so seldom now."

"They're still the best maps of the United States I've

ever seen," Jessie said. "I wish I'd had them when I was studying geography in school. I'd certainly have had a lot easier time and learned a lot more as well."

Ki was studying the map as Jessie spoke. He placed a finger on the upper right-hand corner and said, "The Black Hills start here and they're certainly not cattle range country. But there's a hundred miles of good range west of them, all the way to the foothills of the Big Horn Mountains, and there's prairie to the south, all the way into Colorado."

"Don Carter's spread starts somewhere along the foothills of the Big Horns," Jessie said thoughtfully. "But I'm not sure exactly where it is."

"And I've just noticed something, Jessie," Ki remarked. "There really isn't much cattle range in Wyoming. At least, there's nothing like the amount I'd always imagined there was. Look at this map again." He tapped the areas with a fingertip as he spoke. "Here's an eastern strip between the Black Hills and the Big Horns, and here's another strip near the Medicine Bow Mountains in the south."

"And the rest is mountains," Jessie said. She nodded thoughtfully, tapping the atlas with the folded sheet of paper she'd taken from between its pages. "Yes, you're right, Ki. I thought there was more open range in Wyoming, too."

"What's that you're holding?" Ki asked.

"Oh, I suppose it's notes of some sort that Alex made when he was studying these maps." Jessie unfolded the paper and glanced at the lines written in Alex Starbuck's script. A frown grew on her face as she read.

"Something interesting?" Ki asked her.

"Interesting," Jessie murmured, her eyes still on the small, neat script. "And alarming, too, in a way."

"What way?"

"Listen to what Alex wrote about the Wyoming Territory, Ki," Jessie said. She read:

IT IS A MATTER OF CONCERN TO ME THAT NO ONE IN THE FEDERAL GOVERNMENT SEEMS TO HAVE REMARKED ON THE STRATEGIC IMPORTANCE THE WYOMING TERRITORY HOLDS IN RELATION TO THE RICHEST AND MOST PRODUCTIVE AREAS OF THE CENTRAL AND WESTERN UNITED STATES. AN EXAMINATION OF THIS MAP REVEALS AN EXTREMELY IMPORTANT FACT. THREE OF THE NATION'S GREATEST RIVER SYSTEMS HAVE THEIR HEADWATERS WITHIN THE BORDERS OF THE WYOMING TERRITORY. THESE ARE THE MISSOURI, THE COLORADO, AND THE COLUMBIA. THE MISSOURI, WITH ITS TRIBUTARY, THE PLATTE, PROVIDES AT LEAST HALF THE WATER NEEDED FOR THE MISSISSIPPI TO MAINTAIN ITS FLOW. THE COLORADO IS THE CHIEF WATER ARTERY FOR THE SOUTHWEST. THE GREEN RIVER IS THE MOST IMPORTANT TRIBUTARY OF THE COLUMBIA, ON WHICH THE PACIFIC NORTHWEST RELIES. SHOULD A METHOD BE FOUND TO BLOCK OR DIVERT THEIR TRIBUTARY STREAMS, THE FLOW OF THESE GREAT ARTERIES THAT ARE SO VITAL TO NAVIGATION, FARMING, AND MANUFACTURING COULD BE REDUCED TO A MERE TRICKLE, CAUSING GREAT DAMAGE TO THE ENTIRE NATION.

As Ki began to grasp the meaning of what Jessie was reading to him, he moved to stand beside her at the desk where Alex's atlas lay open. While she continued to read, he bent over the map and with his forefinger began tracing the courses of the headwater streams that Alex had named. When she finished reading her father's note, he looked up from the book with a frown.

"Alex was looking pretty far into the future when he wrote that," he commented.

"He was always aware of the future, Ki," Jessie said. "He foresaw that wooden ships were doomed, that railroads were going to open a fresh flow of commerce, and that a lot of other things would come about. I think he was probably right about these rivers, too."

"He could very well be," Ki said.

"And if Alex could see something like this, others can see it, too," Jessie added.

"Others who don't have anything but their own selfish interests in mind," Ki said.

"Yes," Jessie replied, "I guess my father's remarks explain why the cartel is showing such a sudden interest in the Wyoming Territory. And I'm sure he left another clue that could tell us if we're right."

Jessie moved around the desk to one end and reached between its back and the wall. There was a sharp metallic click and a hidden panel in one end of the desk swung open. Reaching into it, Jessie took out a small, thick notebook. Its pages were dog-eared from much handling.

Ki did not need to ask her about the book; he remembered it very well from the days when he'd been serving Alex. The book contained Alex's private list of known and suspected members of the cartel, not only in the United States, but in Europe as well. He watched with interest as Jessie moved to the nearest chair, sat down, and began thumbing through the pages.

"I thought we might find something here," she said as she stopped at a page and scanned it quickly. "Ki, do you remember the name of that English nobleman Don mentioned when he was telling us about trying to buy land down in the southern part of Wyoming?"

"Of course," Ki answered. "Herrington or Harrington. Don wasn't sure which."

"It's Harrington," Jessie told him without taking her eyes from the page she was reading. "And he's an earl, which puts him quite high in the British peerage. He's also the owner of about half the steel mills in England. And he has a big ranch in Colorado; I suppose he runs cattle on it."

"Most of the Englishmen who buy ranches here in the west do make some kind of show that they're working them," Ki said. "But most of them have more money than they know what to do with and treat their ranches like toys."

"I think we can take the steel mills as a good indication that Lord Harrington doesn't have to depend on cattle ranching for his income," Jessie said and smiled. "And, of course, the steel mills are pretty much a giveaway. We've both noticed that the Europeans in the cartel seem to favor heavy industry."

"If this Harrington is on Alex's list, I think we can be sure he's a key member of the cartel," Ki said soberly. "Alex didn't put any names he wasn't sure of in that book."

"Of course," Jessie stated. "So our suspicions seem to be correct." She closed the book and took it back to its hiding place. As she closed the secret panel and turned back to Ki, she went on, "We'll have to find out more about Lord Harrington and the people he's close to in Wyoming. But first we need more answers from Don Carter."

"Well, I don't know what kind of answers you want, Jessie, but I'll sure try to give them to you if you'll just ask the questions," Carter said from the doorway.

"Don!" Jessie exclaimed, turning from the desk when she heard Carter's voice. "You ought not be on your feet! You're supposed to be in bed resting."

"I don't feel like resting, Jessie," Carter replied. "I tried to sleep, but I couldn't, so I thought I'd get up and move

30

out to the old bunkhouse. I don't want to be getting in the way here."

"You're not," Jessie assured him. "But if you feel you'd be more comfortable out there, I won't try to get you to change your mind."

"It's more like what I'm used to," Carter said. "I know you and Ki are busy, and I don't want to put you to any extra trouble, even if I'm only going to be here a day or so."

"You'd better plan to stay until that bullet hole in your back is healed, Don," Ki suggested. "If Jessie hadn't happened to find you, there's a chance you could've bled to death lying there by the trail."

"I'll have sense enough to keep my bandage on this time, Ki," Carter said. "But I've got to get back up to my ranch. The hands I've got working for me are real dependable, but I'll still feel better if I'm there to keep an eye on them."

"Stay two or three days," Jessie urged. "I feel responsible for seeing that you're able to travel before you think about leaving."

"I guess a day or so won't make all that much difference," Carter said. "And I've got to admit, I'm still a little bit shaky on my feet."

"Good." Jessie nodded. "Now, as long as you're here, I'd like to ask you a few questions, Don. Sit down and tell me what you know about this Englishman who was trying to buy that land you wanted up in Wyoming."

"You mean his lordship?"

"Harrington, I think you said it was," Jessie prompted.

"What is it you want to know about him, Jessie?" Carter frowned. "Because I don't know much myself."

"We know he has a ranch in Colorado," Jessie said. "Do you know where it is? How big it is?"

"Well, I found out that much. His spread's a little ways east of Colorado Springs. I guess you already know that's the area south of Denver where a lot of Englishmen have bought land."

"I know that much," Jessie nodded.

"Then you know about as much as I do, Jessie," Carter said. "I didn't have time to stop off in Colorado Springs on my way down here, but I can do it on my way back if you think it's important. I'd like to know more about this Lord Harrington myself. I haven't given up yet on getting some of that land in the Medicine Bow country for myself."

"You don't have to borrow from a bank, Don," Jessie told him. "I'd be glad to lend you the money you need."

"I appreciate your offer, Jessie, but let me see what I can do at the bank first. And I wish I could tell you more about this Lord Harrington, but that'll just have to wait." Carter stood up. "Now, if I'm going to move out to the bunkhouse, I better get on with it. Unless you've got more questions about Wyoming."

Jessie shook her head. "Not now. But I might have later." When Carter had left, she said, "I think the Circle Star is going to have to get along without us for a while, Ki. What we've found out from Don is a pretty good sign there's something going on in Wyoming that we need to look at."

"I was sure you'd say that," Ki said. "I guess we'll be leaving as soon as Don's wound is healed enough for him to travel?"

"Three or four days, I imagine."

"I'm ready whenever you say, Jessie," Ki told her. "And if we move fast enough now, maybe we can keep the cartel from getting an edge on us."

Jessie, Ki, and Don Carter were in the dining room of the Circle Star's main house just finishing supper when their conversation was interrupted by a knock on the front door.

"I'll see who it is," Ki said, standing up.

"I imagine it's Ed," Jessie said. "I invited him to have supper with us. I thought he and Don might like to compare notes on being foreman of the Circle Star."

"I'll bring him in here, then," Ki told her over his shoulder as he reached the door. "He'd probably like to have another cup of coffee; the hands finished their meal a half hour ago."

"Do that," Jessie said, returning to the half-finished slice of raisin pie that remained on her plate.

"Unless things have changed since I was foreman, Jessie, the hands eat as well as you and Ki do here in the main house."

"I hope they do." Jessie smiled. "You remember what your instructions about meals were, I see."

"After working for the skinflint I left to come here, your orders were about the best I'd heard," Carter replied. "I don't think I'll ever forget them. 'Feed the men the best,' you said. 'If the cook tries to scant the hands, fire him and get another one.' I tell you, Jessie, that was a real treat."

Ki returned before Jessie could respond. He was walking quickly, a frown on his usually impassive face.

"Jessie, I think you're going to have to take a hand in this," he said. "The man at the door told me he's a deputy sheriff from Natrona County up in the Wyoming Territory. He says he has a warrant to arrest Don."

"Arrest me?" Carter blurted out. "What for?"

"Murder," Ki replied.

"Hold on, now, Ki!" Carter protested. "Are you sure the hands haven't rigged up some kind of joke on me? Most of them were here when I was foreman, you know."

"It's not a joke," Ki replied. He turned to Jessie. "What do you want me to do?"

"I'd better go back to the door with you," Jessie told

him. "If it is a practical joke of some kind, we'll find out very fast. If it isn't"—she shrugged—"we'll get to the bottom of this without wasting any time."

"Maybe I'd better go with you," Carter suggested.

"No, Don." Jessie shook her head. "Let me see if I can find out what this is all about. If I need you, I'll call you."

Jessie and Ki started for the door. As they passed through the spacious living room, Jessie said under her breath, "I don't like this one little bit, Ki."

"It seemed a little strange to me," Ki said. "A sheriff in a place as far away as Wyoming wouldn't usually send one of his own deputies such a long distance, even for a major crime like murder. He'd mail an arrest warrant to the local sheriff and have him handle the arrest."

"That's the first thing that occurred to me, too," Jessie said.

They turned into the short hallway, which was really little more than a wide partition designed to shield the spacious living room from a direct blast of the biting wind that in winter often swept across the prairie. A narrow table holding only a lighted lamp stood against the wall opposite the door, and Jessie turned up the wick of the lamp before turning to the door and signaling Ki to open it.

She and Ki looked at the man standing in the doorway. He'd been standing with his back to the door, gazing at the lights that showed in the bunkhouse windows, and he blinked as he turned to face them.

"I'm Jessica Starbuck, the owner of the Circle Star," she told him. "Ki tells me you've come to serve an arrest warrant on one of my guests."

"That's right, ma'am," the man said. "If your Chinee man didn't tell you, my name's Ranse Peters, and I'm a deputy from Natrona County up in the Wyoming Territory."

Jessie was examining him by the lamplight as he spoke.

He could very well have been what he claimed to be, she thought, her eyes flicking over him quickly and taking in details of his face and features.

Peters was a rough individual with a thick, ragged mustache that was only a little darker than his weather-beaten face. Over a blue shirt he wore a vest, but no coat. A badge pinned to the upper left pocket of the vest gleamed silver in the lamplight and glints of brass came from the rims of cartridges in his gunbelt. The belt slanted down on his right side, and the holster in which he carried a Smith & Wesson was lashed to his thigh with a rawhide thong.

"I'd like to see your arrest warrant if you don't mind," Jessie told him.

"Why, sure, ma'am," Peters said. "I'll be real glad to oblige you."

He took a thick fold of papers out of the pocket to which his badge was pinned and handed it to Jessie. She took a step back toward the table where the lamp stood and began to unfold the papers.

Ki was standing at the edge of the open door. When Jessie stepped back, he shifted his position slightly to be able to see both her and Peters. As Ki moved, Peters dropped his hand toward his revolver butt and at the same time kicked the door open wider with his heavy boot.

"Look out, Jessie!" Ki called as he launched himself toward Peters. "This man's a fake! It's a trap!"

Chapter 4

As quickly as Peters' hand was darting for the butt of his revolver, Ki moved even faster. He slammed the door against Peters. The impact of the massive door started the gunman staggering backward, forcing him off balance and ending his effort to draw.

Before Peters had recovered from the impact of the heavy door, Ki opened it wide and half whirled into into a high kick that sent the side of his foot smashing into the phony deputy's jaw.

Peters' head snapped back and his hat flew off. Though he was still trying to get his right hand on his gun, Ki's kick forced him to bring his arms up and spread them. He waved them in the air like thin featherless wings, trying frantically to keep himself from falling.

When Peters staggered backward and began flailing the air with his outstretched arms, Ki pressed his attack. Flashing through the doorway, he swept his foot up in a low kick that struck the man's right knee and sent him sprawling on the hard ground beyond the door.

Pouncing on the prone man, Ki grabbed Peters' right wrist and pulled it up into the small of his opponent's back and then gave Peters' left arm the same treatment.

Clamping one muscular hand around Peters' wrists, Ki used his free hand to push Peters' face into the dirt. Peters tried to shout, but Ki only pushed harder, and the prone man's stream of protest and angry oaths was smothered into almost inaudible, garbled muttering.

Ki was still holding Peters when Jessie stepped out of the house carrying a Winchester she'd taken from the rack that stood beside the front door. In the light flooding from the doorway, she saw the recumbent gunman, Ki still kneeling on his prisoner's back. Jessie took another step, which brought her to their side.

"I thought you'd probably have him tamed by now," she told Ki. "Let's get him inside and see if Don knows who he is."

Tightening his grip on Peters' wrists, Ki heaved his captive to his feet. Peters began trying to talk, but his mouth was full of dirt and gravel, and he managed only a muted squawk. He began gagging and spitting, but still had not recovered the use of his voice when Ki marched him through the door. Jessie closed the door and threw its massive bolt.

"Take him into the study," she said. "I'll get Don and we'll try to get to the bottom of this."

Peters had worked most of the dirt out of his mouth by the time Jessie and Don Carter came in. Like Jessie, Carter had taken a rifle from the rack. Peters' voice was still an unintelligible croak when he first tried to say something as he saw Jessie and Carter entering the study.

"Be quiet!" Jessie snapped unsympathetically. "You'll

have a chance to talk later—after you've answered some questions."

Peters tried to reply, but when he opened his mouth and took a deep breath, he began coughing and wheezing again.

"Bring him a glass of water from the dining room, Don," Jessie said. "But take a good look at him first and tell me if you've ever seen him before."

Carter had been looking at Peters from the moment he and Jessie entered the room. He shook his head. "Not that I can recall, Jessie. Of course, I get a pretty steady stream of drifters at the ranch, all looking for jobs or a meal to tide them over to their next stop. They look about the same, and for all I know, this fellow could've been one of them."

Carter left to get the water, and Jessie said to Ki, "I don't think he'll give us more trouble, Ki. Take his gun and let him sit down."

Ki took his prisoner's revolver from its holster and laid it on Alex's desk. Peters seemed glad enough to settle into the chair Jessie indicated. Ki stayed beside the chair, and Carter returned with a glass of water. After Peters had taken a few swallows and coughed, he turned in the chair to face Jessie.

"It looks like you run things here," he said, "so I'll put you a proposition. Hand over my prisoner and I'll take him away without us having more trouble."

"You seem to be pretty badly mixed up," Jessie replied, her voice icy. "You're the prisoner and will be until you tell us who you are and who sent you here."

"I've already told you that," Peters answered, his voice still rasping hoarsely. "I was sent down here from the Wyoming Territory to bring back a killer who's wanted on a murder warrant."

"And you've lied," Jessie said flatly. "I've looked at

39

that arrest warrant you gave me. It's nothing but a blank form. It doesn't have Don Carter's name on it—or anybody's name, for that matter."

"I guess you just don't understand," Peters told her. "Us deputies don't fill in our warrants until after we've got the crook we're after."

"That's another lie," Jessie told him. "And as far as I'm concerned, it's the last one I intend to listen to. Ki, you—"

Whatever Jessie had intended to say was lost in a clatter and crash as Peters kicked away the chair he was sitting on and leaped to his feet. He'd aimed the chair at Ki, and though Ki reacted instantly by jumping to one side, his quick move did not get him clear of the hurtling chair.

Its legs slewed around, and even though Ki tried to avoid the twisting legs by springing into the air with a leap, the legs crashed into his vulnerable shins. Ki came down to the floor in an ungainly sprawl. His trained reaction was fast, but not quite fast enough. Before he could roll to his feet, Peters was halfway to a window.

Ki dived, his arms outstretched to grab the fleeing man's ankles, but Peters was leaping for the window at the same time. Ki managed to grab one of Peters' ankles. Peters hunched his shoulders instinctively as his head crashed into the windowpane, but he pulled Ki along with him.

Across the room, Jessie and Carter had brought their rifles around when Peters first started his melee, but were forced to hold their fire when Ki rose between them and their target.

After Peters crashed into the windowpane, dragging Ki with him, a rifle barked outside the house, and its cracking report was followed at once by another shot.

The rifle bullets struck Peters. Their impact was enough to slow his forward motion. His body collapsed in midair, his shoulders and chest outside the window, his torso and legs still in the room, and his ankles still gripped firmly in Ki's strong hands.

Jessie and Carter had dropped to the floor an instant after the shots sounded from outside. Jessie began crawling toward the window on the other side of the one Peters had chosen for his escape attempt. Before she reached the window, a rifle spoke outside and the slug crashed through the pane.

"We've got to put the lights out!" Jessie called.

She changed her course, heading now for the desk. When she reached it, she rose to her knees. She was shielded now from the snipers outside by the expanse of wall between the windows. She then got to her feet and blew down the chimney of the light that stood on the desk. The flame flickered and went out.

Carter was already on his hands and knees, making his way toward the table behind the sofa where the room's other lamp still sent out its bright glow. Another shot from outside sent a bullet whistling through the room, and the slug *thunk*ed into the wall above his head as he rose to his knees and reached up to turn out the lamp.

As the room plunged into darkness, the firing outside tapered off and, after a few moments, stopped completely.

"What about Peters, Ki?" Jessie asked.

"He's dead. I'm still holding his ankles, though."

"If he's dead, there's no reason to," she said. "Why not let him drop?"

"I was thinking about what might be in his pockets," Ki replied. "I'll haul him in, though. The way those fellows outside are acting we might be busy for quite a while."

Outside, a fresh burst of firing sounded, but no bullets hit the house. Ki got to his feet and hauled Peters' body through the window. The limp form resisted for a moment, then gave way, and Ki pulled the corpse inside, pushing it up against the wall. The shooting outside grew more intense.

"They're attacking the bunkhouse, too!" Jessie exclaimed.

"And our men are firing back," Ki told her. "Whoever planned this didn't have much sense."

"Just the same, I'm responsible for my men, Ki!"

"Stay here," Ki told her. He did not need to discuss the surprise attack any further. He realized that Jessie knew as well as he did that the raiders could only be hirelings of the cartel. Speaking through the darkness, he raised his voice and called, "Don, you stay with Jessie. I'll go find out what's happening at the bunkhouse and make sure the men stay inside."

"I don't need any help to cover the back of the house through these windows," Jessie broke in quickly. "Don, you go with Ki, cover him while he goes to the bunkhouse, and stay at the front door after he gets back. It won't be long before they'll be coming at us from that side, too, and when they do, we might have to split our force to stand them off."

Ki had started before Jessie was through speaking. When he reached the front door, he waited until Carter caught up with him before blowing out the entry light. The shooting outside had become intermittent now, and he was sure that the hands in the bunkhouse were holding their own.

"I think I've brought you and Jessie a lot of trouble," Carter said, "and I sure didn't intend to."

"Don't worry about it, Don," Ki replied. "Trouble has a way of finding Jessie and me. Now, I know you're not going to shoot at shadows, but don't get nervous and do any shooting you don't have to. You're going to lose sight of me when I cross to the bunkhouse."

"Don't worry, Ki," Carter replied, "I know better than that. But be sure to sing out when you get close to the house on your way back."

Ki opened the door and, in the space of a breath, vanished into the darkness outside.

He heard a rifle bark from a new direction, one beyond the buildings, as he made his way across the area that lay surrounded by the new bunkhouse, the old bunkhouse, and the mess hall. A shot from the back of the bunkhouse replied, and then a spurt of flame and the sound of a rifle shot broke the night. None of the buildings showed a light, which told him that the older hands had reacted to the surprise foray with the speed and skill that came from having survived similar attacks before.

Ki did not slow his pace or alter his course. He reached the side of the bunkhouse and followed it to the corner and around the corner to the door. His eyes had adjusted to the dense darkness of the moonless night by now, and Ki could see that the bunkhouse door was open wide enough to accommodate the barrel of the rifle that protruded through the crack between door and jamb.

Without rising, Ki called softly, "Whoever you are in the doorway, just don't get spooked. This is Ki. I'm coming in."

Silently the door swung open, and the rifle barrel was drawn inside. Ki stepped to the door and slid into the darkened bunkhouse. The faces of the men at the windows showed through the gloom only as vague featureless ovals.

"Ed?" Ki called.

"Right here, Ki," the Circle Star foreman replied.

"Are you and your men all right?"

"Nobody hurt yet. Whoever those snipers are, they're damn poor shots. How about you and Jessie and Don?"

"We're all right."

"How many of them fellows you think are out there, Ki?"

"Eight, maybe ten."

"That's about what I figured," Ed Wright replied. Then he asked, "You need a man or two in the main house?"

"No—not unless they change their tactics and try to rush the house. You can tell by the shooting if that happens."

"We'll be on the lookout," Wright promised. He paused for a moment and asked, "You got any idea what this is all about?"

"Well, you've been here long enough to know about the fight Jessie inherited from her father."

"Oh, sure. But she's real close-mouthed about that. Alex was killed before my time here, and all I know is that whoever killed him seems bound and determined to kill Jessie, too."

"That's about all anybody needs to know, Ed."

"I guess. And I guess Jessie's got her own reasons for not wanting to talk. I sure don't aim to press her none."

"That's the best way to handle it, Ed," Ki said. "Now, since you and the men have things in hand out here, I'm going back to the main house."

Once again Ki traversed the distance by snaking across the bare area between the buildings. The shooting from the perimeter of the buildings had become sporadic now, only an occasional blast spurted red against the black darkness. Ki's eyes were thoroughly adjusted to the night by now, and he saw the door clearly. Carter was still standing in it, his rifle ready, but the main target of the night attackers still remained the bunkhouse.

"Don!" Ki called hushedly as he came within earshot.

"It's all right, Ki," Carter replied. "I can hear you, even if I can't see you."

Carter flinched involuntarily as Ki suddenly stood up less than an arm's length away. Then he asked, "The hands are all right?"

"Ed's got things in good shape," Ki replied, "and I don't think those bushwhackers out there are going to keep shooting very much longer."

"That's my idea, too," Jessie said as she appeared unexpectedly behind Carter, a dark shadow against the white wall opposite the door. "They're already spacing out their shooting."

"I'm sure that means they're getting ready to pull out," Ki said. "And as dark as it is, it wouldn't do us much good to chase them."

"Of course not!" Jessie said. "Even on our own range, they'd get away from us in the dark."

"You're right," Ki said. "And my bet is that they won't all ride off at the same time. If I was handling this raid, I'd leave a couple of men behind to keep letting off a shot now and then. That'd give us the idea the whole bunch is still around."

"They might not be that smart," Carter said.

"No, but if they did that—" Ki stopped short.

When Ki failed to finish what he'd started to say, Jessie said, "You've got an idea, haven't you, Ki?"

"A part of one."

"Go on with it, then," she said.

"If they leave a man or two behind, the way you suggested, I might be able to capture one of them," Ki said thoughtfully. "In the dark, they'd be riding slow. It might be worth trying."

A shot broke their conversation. It came from beyond the bunkhouse, and two shots from the barricaded hands rang out in reply.

Jessie said, "I think they're doing what we thought they would. Whoever fired that shot from the prairie was so far

45

away that we didn't even see his muzzle flash."

"Jessie, I've made up my mind," Ki said. "I want to give my idea a try."

Before Jessie could reply, Carter asked, "Do you really think it'll work? It's as dark as pitch out there."

"No, it isn't really," Ki replied. "Not after your eyes get adjusted to it."

"Ki, I'm not going to ask you to take on a stunt like that," Jessie said.

"I know every inch of the ground for two or three miles around the house," Ki said more to himself than to Jessie and Carter. "Whoever's riding rear for that gang doesn't. And you're not asking me to do anything, Jessie. I'm volunteering. I think it's worth a try."

Jessie hesitated for a moment and then said slowly, "It might be worth it, at that. I'm sure you're able to follow a rider in the dark, Ki, but I can't think of anybody else who could."

"I'll try it," Ki said and he started to turn away.

"Aren't you going to take a gun?" Carter asked.

"You've forgotten, Don," Jessie said before Ki could reply himself, "Ki has his own ways."

"I just spoke without thinking," Carter told her. He turned to say something to Ki, but the spot where Ki had been standing was already vacant.

Before he'd gotten more than a half dozen paces from the house, Ki began trotting in a lope that covered ground quickly without being tiring. His finely honed combat skill was almost a second sense after his years of training in martial arts. He'd remembered the area from which the last shot fired by one of the raiders had sounded, and he headed for it unerringly.

After several minutes passed, the man acting as a guard let off another shot, and Ki altered his course to head directly for the spot where he'd seen the muzzle flash. As faint as the sound of the guard's walking horse was, Ki's keen ears caught the quiet thud of slow hoofbeats from the darkness ahead.

Shifting his direction, Ki headed for the noise. He could still see little in the night's dense blackness, but he knew that his quarry had the same disadvantage. The rider fired again, and Ki closed his eyes too late to avoid having his night vision spoiled by the rifle's blast.

Squeezing his eyes closed but without slowing his steady trot, Ki held his eyelids tightly shut to help to restore his excellent night vision, but he could still hear the light clopping of hoofbeats ahead and let his ears guide him without slowing his steady pace.

In the darkness ahead the horse ridden by the man who was Ki's quarry snorted. Ki heard the tempo of its hoofbeats speed up and realized that the rider had spurred ahead to catch up with the rest of the gang. Ki opened his eyes. The rider was perhaps thirty yards ahead of him now, visible only as a dark blob that hid a small area of the star-studded sky.

Seeing success in his grasp, Ki depended on the louder thud of the horse's hooves to cover the noise of his own light footsteps. He began running at full speed. Before the horse could carry his quarry out of reach, he closed the distance to a dozen feet and the rider still had not heard him. Then Ki leaped.

Chapter 5

Ki landed on the cruppers of the horse with his arms extended and ready. Even before he'd settled securely on the horse's rump, his arms snaked around the rider's neck, and he clamped them tightly in a choke. The gunman dropped his reins to claw at Ki's arm, but Ki had locked in his hold. The big muscle in his left forearm was pressing against his antagonist's windpipe. His right hand was clasped around the man's left wrist, pulling the forearm back to close the rider's windpipe.

For a moment or two the rider pried at Ki's arm, but as the seconds ticked away and his efforts continued to be futile, the outlaw's frantic struggles became feeble and sporadic. Ki did not let up the pressure of his choking hold. The man tried to lean forward in his saddle in order to pull free, but Ki held him firmly erect. The cruel pressure did its work quickly. In a few moments the outlaws's efforts ended suddenly as his body sagged in the saddle.

When Ki was sure the man was totally unconscious and would stay that way for some time, he relaxed the pressure of his arm. Although the rider was unconscious, his body's reflexes did their work, and after a few shuddering gasps, he started breathing shallowly. The horse had slacked its pace after Ki's weight was added to its load, and it slowed still more when its rider stopped spurring it ahead. The animal was now plodding over the dark prairie at a slow walk.

Ki reached around his prisoner's unconscious form and ran his hand along the saddle until he reached the horn. As he'd expected, the outlaw had followed the habit of horsemen and had knotted the reins together so that when they were dropped they would catch on the saddlehorn.

Lifting the reins free, Ki pulled up the horse and slid off its rump. Still holding the reins, he grabbed the arm of the unconscious outlaw as his feet hit the ground and let the man slip out of the saddle. As the rider's limp form sagged, Ki supported the unconscious man and felt his neck. As he'd expected, the outlaw was wearing a large bandanna as a neckerchief. He made quick work of rolling the big handkerchief into an improvised cord and tied his captive's wrists behind his back.

Tossing the outlaw across the horse's withers, Ki swung into the saddle and reined the animal around. At the prodding of his toe, the horse started toward the yellow rectangles of lamplight that were now shining from the windows of the bunkhouse and main house of the Circle Star. Ki's chase and capture had taken less than a quarter of an hour.

"I should've known you'd do what you set out to, Ki," Jessie said when Ki marched his conscious captive into the study where she and Carter were sitting. "Have you had a chance to ask him any questions yet?"

Ki shook his head. "He was unconscious most of the way back. He asked me where I was taking him, and when I didn't answer after he'd tried two or three times, he gave up."

Jessie turned to the sullen man Ki had brought in. The captive's wrists were still bound behind his back. He stared at Jessie while she examined him. Jessie kept her face as expressionless as the prisoner's as she took in his nose, which was splatted from the impact of fists or in falls from the saddle, his tanned cheeks, his chin, which was three or four days overdue for a shave, and a jagged uneven gash of a mouth. He wore ordinary range clothing: heavy tan trousers, a light cotton shirt worn under a jacket, and saddle boots scuffed from long wear.

"Well," the man finally said defiantly, "I guess you'll know me next time you see me."

"Yes. I intend to be able to recognize you—even after you get out of prison," Jessie replied levelly. "I suppose you've got a name?"

"I don't feel called on to give my name out to just anybody who asks me."

"Then I won't bother to ask you again," Jessie told him. "I can wait to find out until the judge calls you to the dock. I'm sure he'll have ways of finding out what it is. You might even be glad to tell him yourself after you've been locked up in a cell for a while."

"Now, hold on!" the captive protested. "I ain't done nothing to go to jail for!"

"Nothing except attempted murder," Jessie said.

"You'll have a hell of a time proving it!" he retorted. "I was just riding across open range, peaceful as I could be, when this damn Chinaman jumped me and knocked me outa my saddle. Dark as it was, he likely got me mixed up with somebody else."

"We'll leave that for a judge and jury to decide," Jessie told him. "Right now, I'm less interested in finding out who you are than I am in learning who hired you to attack my ranch."

"Lady, I don't know what you're talking about," the prisoner said. "Sure, I heard some shooting going on while I was riding across the prairie. It wasn't none of my business to go butting in, so I just kept moving."

Jessie recognized the stubborness of an habitual badman when she saw it and knew that asking more questions would be a waste of time. She turned to Ki and said, "Search him, Ki. We might find something in his pockets that will give us a lead."

"You've got no right—" the man began to say as Ki stepped up to him. Seeing that his protest was not going to be heeded, he cut it short and pressed his lips together stubbornly.

Ki said nothing, but he grasped one of the outlaw's arms just below his bulging biceps and dug his fingers into the captive's flesh to squeeze the median nerve against the bone over which it passed at that point. The captive withstood the pain for a moment, and then tried to jerk his arm free, but Ki held his grip without letting up on the pressure he was applying.

Thrusting out his jaw, the prisoner said, "I don't give a damn what you do to me. You ain't going to get nothing outa me!"

Jessie had encountered hardcases before. She said, "Let him go for the time being, Ki. We haven't searched him yet. Let's find out what he has in his pockets before we really get down to making him talk."

Ki released his grip on the prisoner's arm. The man's expression did not change. "Shall I search him, Jessie?" Ki asked.

When Jessie nodded, Ki started emptying the man's pockets and laying their contents on the table. For a man traveling across the deserted prairie, the outlaw's pockets held surprisingly little. One side pocket of his jacket contained a half dozen rifle bullets; the pocket on the opposite side yielded a supply of pistol cartridges. From one trouser pocket Ki took a handful of loose coins and from the left pocket a jackknife. Both hip pockets held folded bandanna handkerchiefs.

"That's all," Ki announced, looking at the scanty heaps on the table. "Before he started out on the raid, he must've gotten rid of anything that might identify him."

Jessie looked closely at the prisoner, who stared back with a sullen face. "He'd never have thought of doing that, Ki," she stated. "But I'll bet that every man of that bunch was ordered to leave behind anything that might have given a clue to where they came from. And there's only one possible conclusion."

Ki nodded. There was no need for Jessie to mention the cartel as having been responsible for the foray against the Circle Star.

Don Carter had been keeping himself in the background, watching and listening. Now he said, "I guess you two know what you mean, even if I sure don't. But I got used to that when I was your foreman, Jessie, so I won't ask any questions."

Jessie nodded. She'd moved to the table and was examining the items from the prisoner's pockets. Among the glint of Mexican pesos and two or three half eagles, she saw the gleam of base metal. When she spread the coins out with her palm, the brass piece stood out in sharp contrast to the others.

Jessie picked it up, studied both sides briefly, and then passed the medallion to Ki. He read the stamped inscription on one side: HAPPY DAYS SALOON—Cheyenne, Wyoming Territory. Then he turned it over and read the other side: Have One On Us At Molly's Place.

"He might not call Cheyenne home," Ki commented, "but I'd say he's been there not too long ago."

"That's my feeling, too, Ki," Jessie said. She turned back to the captive, who met her look with a defiant tightening of his jaws. Jessie added, "You might as well start talking. We've got a pretty good idea who you're working for."

"All you're doing is guessing, lady," the outlaw said. His voice held more assurance now. "Sure, I been to Cheyenne, but there ain't no law against that."

"No, I don't suppose there is," Jessie said. Turning back to Ki, she said, "Keep his ammunition, Ki, and give him back his money and the rest of his stuff."

"You're going to let him go?" Don Carter asked. His voice showed his surprise.

"We don't have any evidence against him, Don," Jessie said. "We don't even know his name. I suppose that Ki could make him tell us that much—"

"Like hell he could!" the prisoner interrupted. "I can keep my mouth shut from now till doomsday!"

Jessie paid no attention to the interruption. "We're sure he is one of the raiders, but we can't prove it. You know how far we are from the county seat out here on the ranch, Don. If we took him in and asked the sheriff to lock him up, all we'd be doing is wasting two days."

"I guess you're right," Carter stated. "But it doesn't seem right to let him get off scot-free."

Turning from the table where he'd scooped up the outlaw's money and other possessions, Ki said, "it's not right, Don. But what Jessie said is true." He untied the man's wrists and handed him his belongings. "But maybe we'll have another chance at this fellow, and if we do, I intend to see that he doesn't get off so lightly." Ki tilted his head to look up at the man he'd captured. "Now, mount up and don't stop riding until you're off the Circle Star."

Grinning broadly, the man took his time in putting his money back in his pocket and replacing his neckerchief. He made a mocking bow toward Jessie, then turned, and left.

"I don't know whether he realized we'd learned what we needed to know from that saloon token in his pocket," Jessie said to Ki. "But now that we know our suspicions are right, I don't see that there's anything else for us to do."

"When do we leave?" Ki asked.

"In time to catch the evening train," Jessie replied.

"Wait a minute!" Carter broke in. "Where are you and Ki going, Jessie?"

"Back to the Wyoming Territory with you, of course," she said calmly. "I wish we could wait until that wound you've got is completely healed, but we don't have time to waste. There's ugly land grabbing started up there, Don, and we can't let things get too far. We've got to be in Wyoming in time to stop it."

"As far as my bank is concerned, Miss Starbuck, your word is enough to satisfy us," the president of the Cheyenne State Bank said. "Mr. Carter can take possession of that land as soon as the present owner signs the title transfer."

Jessie, Ki, and Don Carter had been in Cheyenne three days while Jessie exerted her considerable influence on the banker to sell Carter the land he wanted in spite of the prospective buyer in Colorado.

"That's very nice of you, Mr. Cromwell," Jessie replied, standing up. She turned to Carter and said, "Now we'd better hurry or we'll miss the night train. I'm eager to see your Powder River country after what you've told me about it."

"We've got a way left to go before you'll see it," Carter told Jessie as they left the bank. "The railroad line's still being built north of Casper, so it'll be slow going after we leave the railhead."

"I'd rather look at it from the back of a horse than from the window of a railroad coach," Jessie said, "even if the horse isn't Sun."

"Well, I'll grant you there aren't many like him," Carter said. "It's too bad you couldn't bring him along."

"Oh, Sun belongs on the Circle Star," Jessie said as they reached the hotel. Ki saw them as they entered, and he rose from the chair in the lobby where he'd been waiting.

"I hope you got everything settled," he said.

Jessie nodded. Then, knowing Ki would understand, she said, "The bank and Don and I worked things out just the way I hoped we would."

"There wasn't a hitch, Ki," Carter replied. "You're now looking at a man who owes more money than he ever figured there was in the world."

With a glance at Ki and knowing that he'd get her message, she said to Carter, "I'd much rather see you have the range than that Englishman from Colorado."

Ki nodded and then said, "We'd better finish talking while we have supper. The restaurant here in the hotel's as good a place as any, and the train's not going to wait for us."

As they sat down to supper, Carter picked up the conversation where it had been interrupted in the lobby. "I won't forget how much I owe you for standing behind me, Jessie. I'm going to work every minute to make it on this new range I've got without having to look to you for more help."

"You've proved you can make it by yourself, Don," Jessie told him. "I don't think I'm risking anything by guaranteeing your loan."

By the time they'd finished dinner, the mood of all three was buoyant. Even waiting and standing in the makeshift depot the Great Northern had thrown up hastily to accommodate the few passengers who used the new spur did not dampen their mood. They boarded the train: a dozen boxcars, a couple of flat cars loaded with tracklaying tools, one flimsy, ancient passenger coach with creaking wooden sides, and a battered, asthmatic locomotive.

There were no other passengers waiting, and none arrived during the few minutes that passed after they got on. The engine's whistle sounded, and the couplings rattled as the engineer took up slack. The train moved ahead slowly. Jessie and her companions put their luggage in the overhead racks that ran along each side of the car above the seats. She settled back in the soft light of sunset for the trip to the railhead.

On the upslope that led to the shadowed heights of the Bighorn range that was silhouetted only a few miles away against a darkening sky, the aging locomotive made slow progress. Darkness was settling in when the train reached the long, steep grade that led up the mountain flanks. The grade was steeper than any they'd yet encountered, and they began slowing down as the locomotive struggled against the drag of the heavily loaded boxcars.

"I'm not sure we're going to make it to the top of this one," Jessie remarked to Ki as she peered through the deepening gloom at the rugged terrain.

Ki leaned forward in order to look past her and out the window. The sun had dropped behind the Bighorns by now, but even in the dim twilight, he could see that the terrain was as rugged as any he'd encountered elsewhere. The sides of the irregular cut through which the train now moved duplicated on a smaller scale the jagged fissures and abruptly rising peaks of the mountains that towered beyond them.

"Oh, I don't think we need to worry about that, Jessie," he told her. "This train must be able to get where it's going and then make it back to Cheyenne or the railroad wouldn't be using it."

"Well, as long as we're on it, I guess there's nothing to worry about," Jessie said. She stifled a yawn. "I think I ate too much supper, Ki. I'm getting awfully sleepy."

"Why don't you just curl up on the seat and nap?" Ki asked. "I'll move across and sit with Don."

Carter occupied the seat directly across from the one in which Ki and Jessie sat, and he moved over to the window. Ki sat down and glanced past him and out the window. From his seat on the opposite side of the aisle, he'd been unable to see anything except the flanks of the sharply rising slope into which the road was being carved. Now, from his new vantage point, he had a clear view of the rim of the valley through which the train was passing. The rim of the cut in which the rails had been laid was lower on that side, and beyond it he could see the downslope, which fell away as abruptly as the mountain flanks on the opposite side rose upward.

A little more than a quarter mile up the slope, he saw that the train was overtaking a half dozen horsemen who were riding almost parallel with the tracks. Ki nodded toward them and said to Carter, "There must be some ranches near here. Those fellows look to me like they're a bunch of hands going home to supper."

Carter turned to look at the horsemen and then turned back to Ki. He said, "Not likely, Ki. I don't know of any

58

ranches along this stretch of track. They're all farther east where there's more graze on the range. Likely those fellows are just drifters or maybe some hands that've driven a herd to market."

"They're riding awfully close to the tracks," Ki said. "If I was in their place, I'd worry about the engine spooking those horses."

"They're pretty close, all right," Carter said. "But I imagine the going's easier where the track gangs have been grading for the road."

They watched the riders for a moment longer. The men were traveling in single file now. Suddenly the two in the lead reined their horses across the tracks and vanished. The train was very close to the group now and Ki frowned, wondering what had led the group to split up. Then the answer came to him in a flash.

"Jessie! Wake up! Those riders are getting ready to hold up the train!"

Even as Ki called his warning, the train began slackening speed. Beside him, Carter was trying to open the window and draw his revolver at the same time. Jessie was sitting up now and Ki repeated his warning.

"There's a bunch of riders, six of them, getting close to the train," he said quickly. "They're acting like robbers. We'd better get ready to stand them off."

Jessie had learned long ago to respect Ki's judgment. She said nothing, but answered him with a quick nod. Sliding out of the seat, she started for the luggage rack where she'd put her rifle.

"Does that mean you think they'll be after us, too?" she heard Carter ask Ki.

For a moment Jessie was tempted to tell Carter enough to give him a better idea of their situation, but that would have meant breaking the ironclad rule to which she and Ki had agreed in the early days of their battle with the cartel, the same rule that Alex Starbuck had imposed on himself and Ki: Never mention the cartel or try to explain it or discuss it with anyone else. The temptation was faint and fleeting, and she thrust it aside at once.

"Of course, they'll be after us!" she replied, her voice sharp in spite of her effort to control it. "There's only this one passenger coach, and they're certainly not after the tracklaying tools that're in those flatcars!"

Chapter 6

Ki glanced quickly around the coach and said, "We can't let them pin us down in here. The walls of this old car won't stop a bullet, and two of them can handle the engineer and fireman. That leaves four to come after us."

"You're right, Ki," Jessie said. "We'd be fools to stay in here and get pinned down." She glanced out the window and went on, "If we get on that slope, we'll be above them."

Ki glanced out the window and nodded. On the steep slope that rose a few feet from the tracks, one or two determined defenders could hold off a dozen well-armed men and keep them from mounting it.

"We're almost going slow enough now for it to be safe to jump," Carter said. "In another couple of minutes, we'll be standing still."

"We'd better move fast!" Jessie warned.

Ki said quickly, "Don, you go first; then you'll be able to give Jessie a hand. I'll jump last."

"All right," Carter agreed. "Let's jump! We're almost standing still right now!"

Groans and creaks were mingling with the sounds of steel wheels grinding on steel rails as they reached the car's vestibule. Carter leaped to the shelving bank, an easy jump, and turned to help Jessie.

She stood poised in the doorway for a moment and then jumped—her rifle in one hand and her free hand extended to grasp the hand Carter was extending toward her.

At the same moment that Jessie reached to grasp Carter's hand one of the riders appeared around the rear end of the moving coach. He was holding his rifle across his saddlehorn, but he made no effort to raise it when he saw Jessie in midair and Carter reaching to take her hand. Instead, the approaching man toed his horse to a faster pace.

Still in midair when she caught sight of the rider, Jessie instinctively turned her head to get a clear view of him. Carter saw Jessie looking back and half turned to see what had drawn her attention.

Both Jessie and Carter realized their mistakes too late to correct them. Jessie missed Carter's outstretched hand and Carter did not step up in time. When he did grab for her hand, he'd waited too long and failed to catch it. Jessie fell forward against him as she landed and sent both of them toppling to the ground.

At the same time that the approaching rider saw Jessie and Carter tumble to the ground, he also caught sight of Ki emerging from the vestibule and planting his feet on the steps of the slowly moving coach. Although he was within a few feet of Jessie and Carter, the man elected to move on Ki. He toed his horse ahead.

Ki's view of the slope where Jessie and Carter lay was indistinct until he stepped forward to make his own jump. He saw the rider for the first time when he glanced to see how his companions were faring. By then the approaching horseman had already ridden past their sprawled forms and was between them and Ki. Then, with a grinding of brakes from the engine added to the coach's creaking, the train at last came to a halt.

Preparing for his leap, Ki had planted his feet firmly on the steps and was hunkering down to jump. His muscles were taut. The instant he saw Jessie and Carter lying prone, he decided that since he had no chance to swivel and attack the rider, he had no alternative but to go ahead with his jump. He dived off the steps toward the slope.

By now the rider was little more than an arm's length away. Just as Ki launched himself, the horseman swung his rifle around like a club. The barrel landed with an ugly *thunk* on Ki's unprotected head and his jump was never completed. Knocked unconscious by the rifle barrel, he dropped like a stone and fell in an ungainly sprawl to lie motionless between the rails and the foot of the upgrade.

Seeing Ki fall, the rider turned in his saddle. He swung his rifle toward Jessie and Carter, trying to get one of them in his sights, but he could not twist his body around far enough. He slid from the saddle and planted his feet, bringing up the rifle as he moved, trying again to get a sight lined up on Jessie and Carter, but having trouble doing so in the fading, uncertain light.

Carter twisted his body as he fell. He landed on his back, and as he started to get on his feet, a pang from the half-healed bullet wound stabbed him. Ignoring the pain, he picked himself up and went to help Jessie.

Jessie had landed on her hands and knees, but had been forced to drop the rifle in order to cushion herself with her hands and arms when she hit the ground. She was scrambling toward her weapon, but it was not yet within reach.

As the noise of the train stopped and she heard the crack of the rifle hitting Ki, she glanced around in time to see

63

him fall senseless to the right of way between the rails and the slope. Abandoning her effort to reach the rifle, she drew her Colt.

Beyond her, Carter was pushing himself to his feet. In spite of the biting pain in his back, he whipped out his own revolver just as he saw two more horsemen coming around the end of the train. One of the approaching riders caught sight of him, brought up his rifle, and shot, but the dusk was deepening into night now and made aiming difficult. The bullet plowed into the ground a few inches short, sending up a little shower of pebbles and dust.

Carter abandoned the nearest man as his target and shot from the hip at the two approaching men. It was an un-aimed shot and his hand was unsteady because of the pangs that were stabbing into his shoulder blade. The slug from the pistol went wide, missing both men. The rider in front had his rifle shouldered by now and was swinging it for a shot.

Carter fell backward with a fraction of a second to spare. The rifle bullet zipped over his prone form with a buzz like that of a giant hornet before singing in ricochet off one of the boulders behind him. As he struggled to get up, the pain in his back wrenched him again, but he managed to get on his feet.

While Carter was swapping shots with the approaching riders, Jessie had drawn her Colt and brought it around. She triggered off a shot at the man who'd brought Ki down. He saw her movement and flattened himself out in the instant it took her to squeeze off a shot. The bullet cut the empty air above the man and plowed into his horse. With a shrill neigh of pain, the animal reared, turning on its hind legs as it rose. Then, as its forefeet landed on the ground, it bolted.

Still neighing with pain, the horse dashed down the narrow space between the tracks and the bluff. Its hooves barely missed Ki.

There was no place for the two men who were approaching to go. They had no room to rein away from the pain-crazed horse, but managed to leap from their saddles before the bolting animal collided with one and then the other of the riderless horses.

Confused by the commotion, the two other animals reverted to their instinct to herd. Rearing, they turned to follow the wounded horse as it dashed across the tracks and down the side of the shallow basin beyond.

Her voice urgent, Jessie called to Carter, "Come on! We've got to find a place to hide!"

"But, Ki's—" Carter began to say.

"We're not going to abandon him," Jessie replied. "We'll go just far enough to find a place where they can't see us and look for a chance to get Ki out of their hands."

As in all mountainous country, the twilight had been short. Night's gloom was deepening faster as Jessie and Carter started looking for a place to hide. The pain in Carter's back was constant now. He could feel his shirt sticking to the wound, and he knew that it had reopened. They were fortunate in their search, though. After going only a few steps up the slope, they came upon a rock outcrop that was so broken and ridged that they could crouch into a space between two narrow, rising ridges and be reasonably safe from discovery.

After they'd settled into the concealment of the little crevice, they discovered that they could still hear the voices of the men who'd attacked the train. Three men were talking loudly and at the same time.

Keeping her voice low, Jessie told Carter, "Don't get the idea I'm not worried about Ki, Don. I am. We've got to find a way to get him back."

"Saying it is going to be easier than doing it," Carter said soberly, managing to keep his voice level in spite of his pain. "There are six of them scattered around that train, and they've got rifles as well as their handguns."

Jessie remembered then that in their need to move quickly she'd left her rifle lying on the slope below. For a moment she thought of retrieving it, but while she was debating the wisdom of such a move, a new voice cut through the confused babble that had been assailing their ears from below. The man's words, clearly audible in the rock crevice, reminded Jessie of the precarious situation she and Carter were in and underlined the plight they were facing.

"What have you three been doing?" the new arrival asked, his heavy voice grating angrily as the three who'd been arguing fell silent.

"We got one of 'em, Manny. The Chink. He was—"

"Damn it, we're supposed to bring back all three!" Manny retorted. "Where are the other two?"

"Up the side of the mountain," another replied.

"I figured that out for myself, Clint, when I heard you three gabbing," Manny retorted sarcastically. "And Sang's going to be madder than a constipated billy goat if we go back without the two who got way!"

"Maybe we better try to find where they got off to," one of the others suggested. "They couldn't have much of a lead on us."

"Damn it, Posthole! You know what that country up there is like! With dark coming on so fast, we ain't got a chance to find the other two," Manny retorted.

"Well, it looks like Sang's just gonna have to be mad, then," the third replied. "But dark or no dark, if you say we got to look, we'll do it. Maybe we can get some lanterns from the trainmen."

"Lanterns won't help, Case," Manny said. "I've hid out

in this country enough to know you got to have daylight to see good if you're looking for something."

"Well, what're we supposed to do, Manny?" Case asked. "Far as I'm concerned, all we can do is take this Chink we got and lug him back with us. At least we got somebody to give Sang."

"That ain't the three he'll be looking for, Case," Manny replied.

"It's better'n none," Case retorted.

"I guess you're right," Manny replied after a moment of silence. "One's better than none."

"What about them two railroaders up in the locomotive?" Posthole asked.

"Leave 'em, Posthole," Manny replied. "They ain't the ones we was sent out for. We'll let the steam outa the boiler and cylinders. Before they can get up enough to start moving again, we'll be halfway back to the hole."

"You mean we ain't going to try to get the Starbuck woman and that other fellow?" Clint asked.

"Suppose you tell me how we'd go about doing that?" Manny shot back sarcastically. When the other man made no reply, he went on, "Them two's still a long ways to go. We can start out afresh and catch up to 'em if Sang says to."

"Manny's got the right idea," Case said.

"I say we do it," Posthole urged. "Hell, we done the best we could."

"Then you can be the one to tell Sang that," Clint snapped. In a milder voice, he went on, "All right. I got sense enough not to argue no more. Let's do it Manny's way."

Crouched in their hiding place, Jessie and Carter remained silent. The night had settled in, but the moon was in its wane and visibility was very poor. They could see the men

67

only as dim shadows as they picked up Ki and started carrying him toward the locomotive.

"That's Ki they're carrying!" Jessie exclaimed. "Come on, Don! We've got to try to get him away from them!"

Carter started to get up, but when he tried to rise to his feet, a fresh sharp pain stabbed him and he fell back.

"What's wrong?" Jessie asked.

"I think that bullet hole in my back opened up when I jumped off the train," he said.

"Let me look at it," Jessie said, "or at least feel it. I can't see much in the dark."

She kneeled by Carter and helped him to sit up. Her hand encountered the unmistakable warm stickiness of freshly drying blood as she pulled his shirt up. Her fingers told her that the old wound was indeed bleeding and she shook her head.

"It's opened again, all right," she told Carter. "And there's not much I can do for it." After whipping off her neckerchief, Jessie folded it into a thick pad and slid it under Carter's shirt to cover the wound. "We'd better stay here," she said. "I don't think there's much we can do to help Ki, not with the odds we've got against us. Do you think you can walk?"

"I'll manage," Carter told her. He started to get up, but when his back muscles tensed, the pain stabbed him again, and he fell back with a groan. He said, "I don't think I can make it for a while, Jessie. I'm sorry, but—"

"Never mind," she broke in. "You'll be all right here, and those men carrying Ki have had enough start so they won't hear me. I'm going to follow them to the head of the train. From the way they talk, they don't intend to waste any time looking for us. I'll work up here above them, and I might see a chance to get Ki away from them."

"You'll need your rifle if you're going to have any sort

of chance to get Ki back," Carter pointed out. "Do you think you can find it in the dark?"

"I'll try," Jessie said. "Will you be all right here by yourself?"

"Don't worry about me," he told her. "Go see what you can do for Ki."

Retracing her steps as best she could in the dark, Jessie moved downslope to the edge of the cut above the tracks. From above and in the dark and with the passenger coach now fifty yards away from the place where they'd jumped out, nothing looked the same. Moving slowly, she explored the rough ground until she came upon the gun. She picked it up and started finding her way in the darkness along the slope until she saw the glow of lantern light ahead. Then the black bulk of the locomotive loomed against the star-studded night sky.

As she drew closer to the locomotive and overheard the conversation of the engineer and fireman, Jessie soon realized that she'd arrived too late.

"I still say we ought've tried to fight off that bunch, Lou," one of the railroaders was saying when Jessie got within earshot. "The super's going to be awful mad about this whole affair."

"Let him," Lou snapped. "When I hired on with this damn railroad, it was to be a fireman, not a soldier. I had my fill of fighting during the war, Sim."

"Just the same, we let 'em get away without us lifting a finger to help that Chinee they took. And we still don't know whether or not they had the other two tied up where it was too dark for us to see 'em."

"We're all right!" Jessie called, starting down the slope to the tracks. "But we've got to get some help as soon as we can. One of the men I'm traveling with is lying back beyond the cars with a wound, and I guess you already know those outlaws captured Ki and took him away with them."

"Ki?" the man called Sim asked as Jessie reached the edge of the slope and jumped down the vertical grade to the roadbed. "That'd be the Chinee fellow?"

"Yes. He's my assistant. My name's Jessica Starbuck." She went on, "The man who's hurt is back down the tracks. He's Don Carter. We're on our way to his ranch up in Powder River country."

"Well, I'm Sim Gregson, Miss Starbuck," the railroader said. "I'm the engineer, which means I'm in charge of this train. This is Lou Bacon, my fireman. And I guess we're as sorry about what happened as you are, but there wasn't much we could do to stop those men."

"Me and Sim was in the engine cab the whole time," Bacon said, "looking down the barrel of a pistol. And I'll tell you the plain truth—the hole in the end of that barrel looked as big as a tunnel."

"And it's pretty obvious that you didn't make much of an effort to fight those outlaws," Jessie said, her voice tight.

"Me and Lou didn't hire on to fight," Sim replied. "The only gun the railroad gave us is a rusted-out Remington that's as apt to kill whoever shoots it as it is whoever he's shooting at."

"That's neither here nor there," Jessie said impatiently. "Don Carter needs to get to a doctor, and I've got to find some kind of law officer or organize a posse myself to go after Ki."

"You ain't going to do neither one for a little while, Miss Starbuck," the engineer told her.

"Perhaps you'll tell me why?" she asked tartly.

"I'll do the best I can," the engineer replied. "First thing is, the outlaws made me open all my steam valves before they left. I closed 'em as fast as I could, and Lou's been

70

cramming the firebox full, but it's going to be a little while before we can roll again."

"I see," Jessie said.

"And the second thing is, we're out in the middle of nowhere. This is a new railroad line, Miss Starbuck. You won't find any towns along it because there hasn't been time to build any."

"Surely there are settlements somewhere around!" she said. "If there aren't, you wouldn't have any need to build a railroad up here!"

"Oh, there are a few shantytowns here and there, but none of 'em has any lawmen that I know of."

"Where is the closest town?"

Gregson frowned thoughtfully and said, "Looks to me like the best thing you can do is stay on the train till we get up to Casper. It's about as much of a town as there is between here and the railhead, and they've got a town marshal up there."

"Is he the only lawman anywhere along the line?"

"Just about. But there's an army fort just a little ways out from town, and the army's about all there is in the way of law here in this part of the territory right now."

Jessie's incisive mind had been working at top speed during the railroader's explanation. She'd decided on her course of action while he was talking. With a decisive nod, she said, "Very well. If one of you will go back with me to get Don Carter to the train, we'll go on to Casper. I'm not going to rest until I get Ki back from the renegades who captured him. Now, Mr. Gregson, let's stop talking and start moving!"

★

Chapter 7

"I'm real sorry now that I got you into all this, Jessie," Don Carter said as they left the doctor's office in Casper. "I sure didn't figure it'd turn out to be such a mess."

Carter's left sleeve had been folded upward, the cuff pinned to the shoulder, and his left hand stuck out between two of the front buttons. The shirt concealed the bandage that the doctor had put on him, a corsetlike wrapping that had been brought up over his left shoulder and around his upper arm to bind the arm firmly against his ribs. A sling under the shirt supported his forearm and hand.

"It certainly isn't your fault, Don," Jessie said. "When you come right down to it, if you hadn't been trying to help me, you'd never be in the fix you are. In a way I feel that I'm responsible."

"Now, Jessie, I don't feel like you're one bit to blame," Carter said quickly. "The thing that bothers me is, what're we going to do now?"

"We aren't going to do anything," Jessie answered, her

voice firmly determined. "You're going to do what the doctor told you to—go back to your ranch and let that wound heal."

"And you figure to go after Ki by yourself? I can't let you do that, Jessie! If you go, I'm going with you!"

"You most certainly are not! I'm not going to be even partly responsible for turning you into a lifetime cripple, and that's what the doctor warned you could happen if you didn't follow his orders."

"But you can't just ride out by yourself to look for Ki!"

"I don't intend to," Jessie replied. "I'm going right now to talk to the town marshal and see if he doesn't know of a man or two I can hire to go with me."

"And where are you going to start looking?" Carter asked as Jessie stopped at the corner and looked down Center Street in both directions. "You don't have the ghost of an idea where that bunch of outlaws took Ki!"

"Right this minute, I don't," Jessie admitted. "But I hope the marshal can tell me where to look or at least give me a place to start from." She pointed to a star-shaped wooden sign that hung over the door of a building on the opposite side of the street. "That must be his office. Come on, Don. Let's go see what we can find out."

After crossing the street, Jessie and Carter took the open door as an invitation and walked into the narrow wooden building over which the sign hung. A tall man, so thin he was almost emaciated, was leaning back in a chair, his booted feet propped up on the top of a scarred table.

"Morning, folks," he said. "You looking for some help from the law or just come in to ask how to get somewhere?"

"Perhaps both," Jessie replied. "You are the marshal here, I suppose?"

"Sure am. Taylor Hart, ma'am. How can I help you?"

"My name's Jessica Starbuck," Jessie replied. "And this is

Don Carter. He has a ranch in the foothills south of Casper, and I'm from Texas. I came in to find out what you're doing about catching a gang of train robbers."

"You'd be the folks that was on that Great Northern train, then," Hart said. "The one some outlaws stopped on the spur the railroad's building up to the main line?"

"That's right," Jessie said. Without waiting for an invitation, she sat down in the chair that stood across the table from Hart. "I hope you're getting a posse together to try to track them down and arrest them."

"Well, now, I hate to tell you this, Miss Starbuck," Hart replied, "but I ain't got no jurisdiction outside of town, and that train holdup was a long ways from Casper."

"But aren't you the only law officer in the area?" Jessie asked.

"I sure am," Hart said. "But that don't give me no ticket to go messing in a crime that took place anywhere else. That's the job of the federal marshal's office, and it's clear down in Cheyenne."

"But those outlaws kidnapped Ki!" Jessie protested.

"He'd be the Chinee man that was traveling with you," Hart said. "I heard about him from them railroad men. They said the Great Northern's detectives would likely go out to try to find him—if they wasn't too busy."

"Look here, Hart," Carter said sternly, "isn't it your job to protect the honest citizens who live here?"

"I guess that'd be one way to look at it," Hart replied. "But like I told Miss Starbuck, if your ranch ain't right here in Casper, it's outa my jurisdiction."

"Isn't there somebody else we can look to for help?" Jessie asked.

"Why, there's them soldiers out at Fort Casper that's supposed to keep the redskins from running wild," Hart replied. "But outside of that, I don't guess there's much of anybody else."

"I'd say the soldiers are our best bet, Jessie," Carter suggested.

"Yes. But I have one or two more questions to ask." Jessie said. Turning back to the officer, she went on, "I heard those men who held up the train talking among themselves about someone they called Sang. Do you have any idea who that might be?"

"Oh, sure," Hart said. "They was likely talking about old Sang Thompson—his real first name's Sanford, but nobody calls him by it."

"Who is he?" Jessie asked. "A rancher?"

Hart shook his head. "Not by the length of a billy goat's whiskers, ma'am. I doubt there's more than ten people in Casper who'd know him if they was to run into him on the street. But everybody knows old Sang's an outlaw. The story is that he mostly rustles cattle now, though."

"And nobody's ever been able to catch him?"

"Not yet. He was pulled in for robbing a bank up in Sheridan one time, but that was eight or ten years back, and they never proved it on him. Just like nobody's ever proved he's a cattle thief."

"He lives around here, then?"

"I don't guess you could say old Sang lives much of anyplace. It'd be closer if you said he spends part of his time hereabouts, mostly up in the hole when he's hiding out from the law."

"That's the other thing I wanted to ask you about," Jessie said quickly almost before Hart had finished his explanation. "Those men I overheard mentioned the hole. It didn't make any sense to me then, and it still doesn't."

"Well, the story goes that Sang's got him a hide-out up around Kaycee. He calls it a hole in the wall."

"Hole in the wall." Jessie frowned as she repeated the phrase. "You know, I've heard of a place by that name

76

before, but it was a good distance west, in Mormon country."

"I've heard about that one myself," Carter broke in. "If I remember, it's supposed to be on the other side of the Rockies from here, on the Green River in Utah Territory."

"And I imagine a man could uncover a few more if he had his mind set on working at it," Hart said. "But this one Sang run into is north of here in the Powder River country, and that's all anybody seems to know about it."

"No one knows exactly where it is?"

"Why, I'd guess there's a lot of people that knows," Hart replied. "Thing is, they ain't talking. Most of 'em is cattle rustlers like him, and the talk is that they run the cattle they've stole into the hole where they rest the steers and change brands and give 'em new earmarks."

"It seems to me like they'd need a place to live themselves if they keep the cattle there very long," Jessie said thoughtfully. "I run a reasonably large ranch myself, and if brands have to be changed they'd have to keep the cattle there until the brands don't look raw and new."

"From the stories I've heard, Sang's got himself quite a little town in the hole in the wall by now," Hart said. "And the valley it opens into is supposed to be pretty large, big enough for some shacks and all that. And I heard there's plenty of good range in it. It'd be a big place, all right. I can't say for certain because I never seen it."

"Is there a town or settlement of some kind close to it?" Jessie asked. "If there's not, where would the outlaws who use it as a hide-out get their supplies?"

"There's a little town about sixty or seventy miles north of here," Hart replied. "It's called Kaycee. From what I been told, that's where the ones who hide out in the hole go to do their trading."

"I don't suppose there's anything more you can tell us

about it, is there?" Jessie asked.

Hart shook his head. "I got a hunch I been talking more'n I ought've already," he told Jessie. "But you got a way of making a man feel like he wants to tell you things, Miss Starbuck."

"I take that as a compliment, Marshal Hart." Jessie smiled as she stood up. "And I think you've helped me a great deal. I thank you."

"My pleasure, ma'am." The town marshal nodded. "And I hope what I told you ain't going to lead you to get into trouble."

"So do I, Marshal Hart," Jessie replied. "But if it does, the trouble will be of my making, not yours."

As Jessie and Carter walked back toward the hotel, he said, "I hope you're not planning to try to get Ki free single-handed. From the way Marshal Hart talked, I got the idea that rustlers and other kinds of badmen are pretty thick all the time in that place they call the hole."

"Oh, I'm sure," Jessie said. "But I'm not foolish enough to go there alone, Don. I'm going to follow your suggestion and enlist the best help I can think of, the United States Army."

"Do you think they'll listen to you?"

"Perhaps they won't listen the first time," she replied calmly, "but I'm sure I can persuade them the second time."

"What makes you think so, Jessie? From what I learned during my army days, I got the idea the commander of a place like Fort Casper pretty much runs things to suit himself."

"Oh, he does. But let's not even step out on that bridge until we get to it. Now, the thing for you to do is to follow the doctor's orders and go back to the hotel and rest. I'm perfectly capable of going to Fort Casper by myself."

For a moment Don looked at Jessie as though he was

going to refuse, but the habit he'd formed of obeying her during the time he'd been foreman of the Circle Star proved too strong. He shrugged, nodded, and turned into the door of the hotel when they reached it. Jessie went on to the livery stable around the corner. The best animal the liveryman had was a far cry from Sun, but Jessie had learned long ago that there was no other horse like the great palomino. She accepted a sturdy Morgan that acted very obediently when the liveryman put him through his paces at her request.

"I'll need a saddle, too," she told the liveryman.

He shook his head and said, "I'm right sorry, ma'am, but we only got one sidesaddle, and it's rented out till next week."

"I don't remember asking you for a sidesaddle," she said. "Just put on the best saddle you have. Now, I'm going back to the hotel and change, and I'd appreciate it if you'd have the horse ready when I get back."

Later, feeling refreshed after the first horseback ride she'd had since leaving Texas, Jessie saw the log stockade and low buildings of Fort Casper rising from the rolling prairie ahead. She splashed across the North Platte at the ford and a few moments later was reining in at the fort.

Fort Casper was smaller than she'd expected it to be. There were fewer than a dozen buildings enclosed by a low log stockade. The buildings were low and squat, and Jessie wondered how a man could stand erect in them. Their walls were built of squared-off logs, and their roofs were of earth packed solidly into dome-shaped humps. The doorways were low, the windows small and glassless, and the wooden shutters that closed them swung outward.

She was surprised to see a sentry pacing back and forth in front of the wide gate that opened into the stockade, and her surprise was even greater when she started to enter and he stepped in front of her and barred the way.

"I've got to ask you to tell me your name and business before you go inside the stockade, ma'am," he said.

"My name is Jessica Starbuck," she replied. "I have business with your commanding officer."

"Maybe you wouldn't mind stating your business, ma'am. The major don't like to be interrupted unless it's important," the sentry said.

"You can tell the major that I've come to ask him for some assistance in recovering a man who's been kidnapped by a band of outlaws," Jessie answered. "And you might add that I'd appreciate his receiving me without any delay."

"Yes, ma'am," the sentry replied. He turned and stepped inside the gate, cupped his hands around his mouth, and shouted loudly, "Officer of the Day!"

Jessie frowned as she took a closer look at the gate. An officer in dress blues, his brass buttons and twin captain's bars shining like mirrors, appeared around the nearest building and hurried to the gate.

"What's the call for, Simpson?" he asked as he returned the young sentry's salute.

"This lady wants to see the major, sir," the sentry said. "Something about outlaws capturing a man she knows."

"Did you get her name?"

"Yes, sir. She said it's Starbuck, sir."

"Starbuck," the captain repeated, raising his head to look at Jessie. "Did she say why she wanted to see Major Halloran?"

"About outlaws capturing somebody, sir."

"Stand easy, Simpson," the captain said. "I think I'd better see what she wants before I disturb the major." Walking up to Jessie, the officer saluted and said, "I'm Captain Kelly, Miss Starbuck. Would you mind telling me exactly what you want to talk to the major about?"

"Just what the sentry told you," Jessie replied. "While

80

my assistant and I were on the way to Casper, an outlaw band held up the train and took him prisoner. Since there's no other kind of law in this part of the Wyoming Territory, I've come to ask the army for help in getting him back."

"I see," Kelly said. "I suppose you've tried to get help from the civil authorities?"

"Captain, if you've been here more than a few days, I'm sure you've learned that there aren't any civilian authorities in this area," Jessie said patiently.

"I'm well aware of that," Kelly said. He then went on, "Let me ask you one question, Miss Starbuck. Your name isn't a common one, and I wonder if you might be Alex Starbuck's daughter."

"Yes, I am," Jessie said. "But I don't see what that has to do with my needing help."

"It was a personal question, Miss Starbuck. My father was lucky enough to be associated with yours in two or three business ventures. He had a very high opinion of Mr. Starbuck, I might add, and always told me I couldn't pick a better man to model myself after."

"And did you?" Jessie smiled.

"I tried, even though I only saw him twice when he was visiting father. But West Point gave me a taste for army life, and I let my younger brother take my place in father's business."

"I see," Jessie said. "Well, Captain Kelly, your story is interesting, and I'm glad your father and mine were friends. But I still need to talk to your commanding officer."

"I'll take you to him right now," Kelly told her. "But I'd better warn you that I don't think you'll have much luck with your request."

"Would you mind telling me why you don't?" Jessie asked as Kelly moved up to hold her stirrup while she dismounted.

Kelly dropped his voice and said, "Major Halloran's a spit-and-polish officer, ma'am. He's just been assigned to field duty here after a hitch as an instructor at the Point. He believes in going by the book, and in his book the army's job here is to keep the Indians from causing more trouble. But maybe you can persuade him to change his mind."

"I certainly intend to try!" Jessie replied. "If the army can't help the people, there's no point in having it."

"I have to agree with you, Miss Starbuck," Kelly said as he offered his arm. "I just thought you'd like to know."

"I appreciate it," she said as they walked around the first building beyond the entry and Kelly stopped in front of its open door.

"I'll have to ask you to wait outside," he told her. "The major always wants to know who's calling on him and about what."

"I understand," Jessie said. "Please go ahead."

When Kelly stood aside and Jessie found that she had to step down to enter the building, she understood why all the fort's structures seemed so squat. The floor had been excavated and stood a good ten inches below the ground level. She looked around the bare interior. The building had been partitioned into two rooms; the outer room in which she stood was furnished with only a desk and two chairs.

In the second room, she could see an officer sitting at a table studying a document of some kind. He looked to be in his middle or late forties and wore the official cavalry whiskers, flowing mustache and heavy sideburns above a clean-shaven chin. Even from the doorway Jessie could see that both the beard and his hair were threaded with gray. He looked up when Kelly knocked and nodded in return to his salute.

"What is it?" he asked.

"A lady to see you, sir. A Miss Starbuck. She's come to

ask for us to help her get back a man who was captured by some outlaws during a train robbery."

"You should know by now what my answer is to that kind of thing," the major said. "Tell her to go to the civilian authorities. Chasing outlaws is not a proper military function."

"Excuse me, sir," Kelly replied. "But I think perhaps it would be wise for you to talk to her. Her late father was very well connected."

"Starbuck?" Major Halloran frowned. "I never heard the name. Go back and tell her what I just told you."

Jessie decided to waste no more time in waiting. She walked quickly through the outer office, brushed past Kelly, and stopped in front of Halloran's desk.

"I'm Jessica Starbuck," she said. "I couldn't help hearing your instructions to Captain Kelly, and I thought you might like to know that before I came out here I tried to find some of the civilian authorities you mentioned. There aren't any. That's why I came to ask the army for some help."

Halloran pressed his lips together, and Jessie could see that he was suppressing his irritation at her interruption. He said, "My instructions stand, Miss Starbuck. I appreciate your problem, but it's not the army's job to chase criminals. We're here to protect the civilian population from the Indians."

"If you'd stopped when you said the army's job is to protect the civilian population, you'd have made more sense, Major Halloran," Jessie told him, holding back her rising anger. "I don't see that it makes any difference whether we civilians are having trouble with Indians or outlaws!"

"Now, listen to me, young lady!" Halloran began.

"No," Jessie broke in, "you listen to me. Unless I get

the help I need from you, I intend to go back to town and send a telegram to President Hayes, with whom I had dinner in the White House less than a month ago. One of the things the President mentioned was his concern that there are too many soldiers at too many forts here in the West now that the Indians are settling down. He said he was faced with the problem of reducing the size of the army now that it no longer has a useful job. I'm sure he'd be interested to know that you don't consider it a useful job to protect people from outlaws!"

Chapter 8

For almost a full minute after Jessie finished speaking, Major Halloran sat staring at her, shock mingling with disbelief on his bearded face. He asked at last, "Do I understand that you claim to be personally acquainted with President Hayes, Miss Starbuck?"

"If you want proof, I'll be glad to send the telegram I mentioned," Jessie said, her voice cool. "I'll even write it and let you have your own telegraphers send it over your army wire if you wish, so you won't think I'm playing some kind of trick on you."

Kelly had started grinning the instant Jessie mentioned the name of the president. He'd managed to erase the grin when Major Halloran glanced at him, but was still having trouble keeping a straight face.

He made another effort not to smile and showed no sign of anything except concern in his voice when he said, "Begging your pardon, but my father was very well acquainted with Miss Starbuck's father. He was a man who exercised a great deal of power. I'm sure Miss Starbuck wasn't just talking idly when she told you her intention of sending a telegram."

"I'll repeat my offer," Jessie said quickly, before Halloran could speak. "If you don't want me to use your army facilities, I'm quite prepared to go back to Casper and send my message from there."

Halloran's voice reflected the wilted look that had formed on his face. He said, "I don't think that will be necessary, Miss Starbuck. You say you want help. Exactly what is it you want me to do?"

"I have a ranch in Texas. I came to the Wyoming Territory to look at some land," Jessie said. "Day before yesterday, while I was traveling from Cheyenne on the new spur the Great Northern's building, a bunch of outlaws held up the train and captured"—she hesitated for a moment as she debated the best way to describe Ki and then went on—"my right-hand man. When I went to the marshal in Casper, he suggested the outlaws had probably taken him to a place called the hole. I suppose you've heard of it?"

"I've not only heard about it, Miss Starbuck, but I'm very well acquainted with it. Or perhaps I'd better say, I'm very well acquainted with the legend that such a place exists."

"I believe you're mistaken in calling it a legend, Major Halloran," Jessie said quietly.

"It's a legend and nothing more," Halloran assured her, confidence in his voice. "I'm positive about that. When I arrived to take command of Fort Casper and found that the men here had been wasting a great deal of time looking for it, one of the first things I did was to put a stop to that frivolous activity."

"I'm sorry your men weren't successful. But what you've said isn't going to change my mind about there being such a place or stop me from looking for it. I owe that much and a lot more to Ki."

"To whom?" Halloran asked, frowning.

"Ki. That's the name of my—well, I suppose the easiest way to explain the work he does for me is to tell you he's my aide-de-camp."

When Halloran heard the familiar term, he relaxed and nodded. "I see." Then he asked, "What gives you the idea that he's in this hole?"

"I could overhear the outlaws talking after they'd captured him. They mentioned it. Not as hole in the wall, of course. But they talked about taking Ki to the hole."

"Which you took to mean hole in the wall?" Halloran inquired. When Jessie nodded, he asked, "And that's all you have to go on?"

"Not quite," she replied. "The outlaws also talked about someone called Sang, and the marshal in Casper later told me that the hole had been discovered by a cattle thief and outlaw called Sang Thompson."

"Miss Starbuck, you're basing your request for me to send out a party of men on a few words you overheard when you were in a situation where you were very tense and excited," the major said. "I still don't—"

Kelly cleared his throat loudly, and when Halloran looked at him, Kelly said, "Begging your pardon, but I have an idea that might help. If I can make a suggestion, sir—" He raised his eyebrows questioningly.

"Go ahead," Halloran stated.

"I have a week of leave coming to me, sir," Kelly replied. "With your permission, I'd be glad to use that time to go with Miss Starbuck and help her try to find her assistant."

"In spite of what you just heard me say?" Halloran asked.

"I meant no reflection on your opinion, sir," Kelly said quickly. "But because my father and hers were friends and business associates, I feel it's my duty to help Miss Starbuck, even if this is the first time we've met."

Halloran was silent for a moment. Then he said, "I find it hard to differ with you, Captain Kelly. If you wish to take your leave and go with Miss Starbuck, I can't object."

Kelly turned to Jessie. "Perhaps I should ask if you want my help before I volunteer it, Miss Starbuck. If you do—"

"I'd be very glad to have you go with me," Jessie said quickly. "You certainly know the country hereabouts, and I'm sure you can save me a great deal of time."

"When would you like to start?" Kelly asked.

"As soon as possible. Tomorrow, if that's not too soon."

"Tomorrow suits me fine," he said.

"I'm staying at the Castle Hotel," Jessie said. "I'll be waiting for you in the morning."

Jessie glanced at the shadow of her horse and knew without looking up at the blazing sun that it was almost at its zenith. Though the morning had been cool, by now ripples of the heat's haze were beginning to form above the short prairie grass. They did not rise high enough yet to cloud the air, but shimmered over the short dry grass that covered the vast saucerlike basin.

As yet the distortion had not risen high enough to hide the eastern upslope, as it would later in the afternoon. Above the distorting air close to the ground, she could see the gentle and seemingly endless rise of the basin's eastern side. At the very edge of the quivering air, Jessie could just make out the tiny, moving dot that was Sean Kelly riding slowly on a course roughly parallel to hers.

Beyond Kelly, the flat grassland was broken by a rough patch of barren ground that surrounded a series of abrupt rises that he'd told her were called Pumpkin Buttes. Even though Jessie was accustomed to the vast expanse of featureless Texas prairie that surrounded the Circle Star, the distances in this part of the Wyoming Territory somehow impressed her as being greater, wider.

This was the second day that Jessie and Kelly had been riding across the great saucerlike prairie since leaving Casper. The connection between Kelly's father and Alex Starbuck had led to an early abandoning of formalities between them. Long before they'd stopped for the night they were using first names, chatting easily like old friends as they rode across the rolling land stretching north from Casper.

"I've already explored just about all this area close to the fort," Kelly had explained. "Or when I've been out leading a patrol I've heard my men talk about how they've combed over it. There's no use wasting our time this far south. Tomorrow and the next day will be when we want to keep our eyes open."

"Everybody seems to know about this hole, but nobody knows where it is or wants to talk about it," Jessie said. "Why is that?"

"I'm not sure my answer's right, Jessie, but I've run into the same thing," Kelly replied. "Sang Thompson's getting up in years now, I suppose, but from the stories I've heard about him he was a deadly killer when he was younger. There aren't too many ranches in this part of the territory yet, and what few there are belong to men with families."

"I see," Jessie said. "Thompson's let the word go out that he'll avenge himself on the family of anyone who gives away his hiding place."

"Something like that," Kelly said. "It's hard to be sure about such things. The best you can do is make a guess about what might've happened in the past."

"It does make sense, though," Jessie said. She smiled to herself as she thought of the side of her life that she did not mention to strangers.

Kelly said, "Lately there've been some hints that Sang Thompson's been letting some of his outlaw friends, rustlers and men on the dodge, use the hole as a hide-out and a place to keep stolen cattle while they change brands and get them ready to sell."

"And, of course, the ones he lets use it would be on his side, ready to help him carry out his threats," Jessie stated, frowning thoughtfully.

"Outlaws stick together," Kelly agreed. "And secrets like the hole can be kept pretty easily in places where there aren't a lot of people."

"And I'd never call this part of Wyoming overpopulated," Jessie said. "Except for those two ranch houses we passed right after we stopped at noon, all we've seen were a few little bunches of steers. This part of Wyoming is very much like my Circle Star country, Sean. It's like it, but it's not the same. I suppose it's the mountains all around us that make the difference."

As they'd started that morning from the little trickle of a stream that Kelly had identified as Sand Creek, he'd pointed to a distant hump and told Jessie, "Suppose you make that your landmark. It's called Teapot Dome because there's a little creek named Teapot Creek on the other side of it. You'll want to stay to the left of it."

"From what I've seen so far, it's the creeks we're interested in more than anything else," Jessie said. "If outlaws are hiding rustled cattle, there'd have to be a stream flowing in it or close to it."

"Of course," Kelly said. "That's why I'm going to angle off to the east." He pointed in a northeasterly direction. "The broken country starts in that direction north of Pumpkin Buttes, and there are a few small streams cutting through it. You'll be able to see the buttes by noon, and along toward the middle of the afternoon, I'll cut west from the buttes to join you in the foothills."

"I suppose there'll be water in the direction I'm going?" she asked.

"Enough so that you and your horse won't be thirsty. I've ridden over that section on scouting trips, and it's not really as bad as it looks."

"Shouldn't we be getting to the Powder River pretty soon?"

"Before dark," Kelly stated. "That's where we'll meet this evening, but at the mouth of Salt Creek. You won't have any trouble finding it. Teapot Creek runs into Salt Creek, and Salt Creek into the Powder. Don't expect it to be much of a river there, though. You'll see a little bit of water in it, but along there the Powder's mostly trickles between puddles."

"I've heard that about the Powder River," she said.

"Yes. It describes the part you'll be riding along. But we ought to join up in time to push on to that little place they call Kaycee if you feel like it."

"I don't know how I'll be feeling this evening," Jessie said. "Let's wait until you join me to decide what to do."

"Fine," Kelly said. "I'll see you this evening."

After they'd separated, Jessie had let her horse set its own pace as she rode across the gently slanting ground toward the landmark Kelly had pointed out. Moving across the brittle crust of the prairie's soil, Jessie scanned the ground, looking for hoofprints that would mark the path a cattle herd had taken.

Jessie hadn't expected to see anything of interest while moving across the level prairie of the basin, so she had not been disappointed when her expectations were fulfilled. She swung around the hump of Teapot Dome and reached the creek that gave the potlike landmark its name. She reined in and let her horse drink before moving on.

By the time she'd reached the juncture of Teapot Creek and Salt Creek, the heat's haze had risen so high that she could no longer see clearly across the vast basin. At what seemed almost an infinite distance because of the haze that filled the lower air, the brown-green tops of mountains were appearing now. She squinted, trying to see the ground and catch sight of Kelly, but he had disappeared below the level of clear air and was hidden by the quivering luster that now formed its lower level.

Although Jessie was in no particular hurry, she decided to eat her lunch in the saddle. Groping in her saddlebags, she found the sack of crackers and dried beef that she'd taken from her share of the rations bought in Casper. She ate as the horse plodded along. Her hunger satisfied, she stowed away the remainder of the food and went back to watching the monotonous strip of creek that was all she could see through the haze.

At some time in the late afternoon, Jessie reached the Powder River. She was not aware immediately that she'd gotten to her objective, for as the air had grown warmer, the haze had risen higher. The shimmering air engulfed Jessie until she'd been able to see only a short distance from the stream along which she'd been riding. Her first realization of her location came when she noticed that her horse's gait was easier, and a few moments later she could tell that she was riding on a downslope.

Reining in, she peered ahead, but the shimmer limited her vision to a quarter-mile at best. Urging her horse ahead, Jessie reined into the bed of the stream. Her horse's hooves sank into soft sand as she looked ahead for the glint of water and saw only the same expanse of dry sand for another fifty or sixty yards. She moved across the sand, trying to pierce the haze in front of her, and at last saw the glint of water. The glint came from a trickle that was barely a yard wide and only a few inches deep.

"It's got to be the Powder River," Jessie said aloud into the silent air. Swinging out of her saddle, she bent and dipped her hand into the water and licked her dripping fingers. The water held no trace of salt. "I suppose I just didn't notice when Salt Creek flowed into it."

Above the flowing stream, the haze did not obscure the air. Jessie peered upstream and down, but could see nothing except the river bed and a small strip of the bank on each side. Then she noticed that the bank on her left was higher than that on the right, and with the idea that the left bank might continue to rise and get her above the haze, Jessie walked the horse to the shore and started ahead again.

As she'd hoped but only half expected, the ground kept rising steadily. Gradually the haze thinned, and on her left side Jessie could see the sharply upthrust face of an almost vertical butte that rose two or three miles ahead and jutted above the haze to a height of a hundred yards or more. She turned the horse toward the butte, and as she got still higher above the layer of shimmering air, she could see a second butte that rose beyond the first and the stretch of gently rising ground that stretched away from them in the direction of the river. Both buttes looked to be of almost equal height, and they were separated by a slit of a valley that cut between them.

Jessie reached the top of the rise and pulled up. She was in clear air now above the haze, which spread across the river bed in a dancing, quivering, impenetrable blanket. In the distance she saw the tips of Pumpkin Buttes protruding above the haze, and she wondered how close Kelly might be to the river. Then she realized that since she'd passed the mouth of Salt Creek, she'd need to retrace her steps to meet him when he arrived.

Unhurriedly, she turned the horse downslope. The animal had taken only a few steps before Jessie snapped alert and pulled back on the reins. The twin buttes were at her back, but she could still see the long stretch of sloping ground that led down to the basin. She could also see the bobbing heads of cattle emerging from the haze that obscured the landscape below.

Easing back in her saddle, Jessie reined in, her interest aroused by the sight of the herd's slow emergence from the haze. She watched the cattle that followed the lead steers as they plodded up the steep slope toward the buttes. In a moment a horseman emerged from the shimmer that obscured the ground. He turned his horse and started hazing the animals in front toward the second of the two buttes. More cattle kept appearing, following the lead steers at an easy diagonal that would take them through the gap between the buttes.

Jessie had joined the Circle Star hands in many roundups and in drives from one section of the vast ranch's range to another, so she recognized the plodding gait of tired steers. To her expert eyes, it was apparent that this herd had been driven very hard for a long distance. Looking at these animals, she saw the slow uncertain steps they were taking and shook her head.

As the parade of cattle dwindled, a second horseman came into sight. He was swinging a looped lariat, trying to get the stragglers to move faster and catch up with the body of the herd. By now the lead cattle were beginning to disappear between the two buttes.

"If those were my steers being driven like that, I'd fire the hand who was hazing them so fast he wouldn't know what hit him," she said under her breath. "They'll need to stop and rest a long time before it's dark enough to bed them for the night. Those hands ought to know enough to let the critters find their own pace. There's no reason to push them that hard unless—"

Stopping short, Jessie watched the steers trickling through the gap between the buttes and then added, "Unless they're trying to hide them. In a place called the hole!"

Chapter 9

For a moment Jessie sat motionless, trying to absorb the discovery she was almost sure she'd made. Then she turned her horse and started it moving down the slope toward the river. She wasted no time now. It was close to sunset, and she did not want Kelly to reach their meeting place first and get alarmed because she was not there.

Going down the slope back to the river took much less time than ascending it. The sky was just beginning to take on a pink tinge above the haze when Jessie reached the place Kelly had set for them to meet. This time she recognized the spot at once; coming from the upstream direction of the river made a big difference.

Jessie saw immediately why she'd ridden past the point where Salt Creek flowed into the Powder; the two streams made their junction at a place where the river dwindled to a thin thread and looped in a zigzag of curves between banks so high and narrow that the creek looked like just another curve in its course.

She reined in and swung to the ground before letting her horse drink. After she'd dropped the animal's reins and knowing it would stand until she picked them up again, Jessie walked upstream a few yards to drink. She was still hunkered down beside the river and cupping water in her palm, when she heard the thudding of hoofbeats. Jumping to her feet, Jessie dropped her hand to the butt of her Colt until she could be sure the rider was Kelly. When she recognized him, she hurried to meet him.

"Have you been waiting long?" he asked as he dismounted.

"Only a few minutes," she said. "I missed the fork and rode past it, which might have been the biggest stroke of luck that will come our way."

Kelly frowned, puzzled. "How's that?"

"Because I think I've found the trail to the hole, Sean! We'll have to go see if I'm right while it's still daylight."

"Suppose you tell me about it first," he suggested.

Jessie told him of her error in going upstream along the river and mounting the bluff where she'd seen the cattle herd being driven into the cleft between the twin buttes.

"Don't you see," she concluded, "Being on the bluff, I was looking at those buttes from an angle that you wouldn't get if you were lower down on the floor of the basin."

"That may be true," he nodded. "I noticed the buttes while I was riding across the basin floor below them, but it looked to me like they were joined together."

"They must not be the same formation, Sean," Jessie said insistently. "I saw those steers disappear."

Kelly glanced at the sky. The western rim of the horizon was a rosy pink, but the disc of the setting sun had not yet touched it.

"We've got two or three hours of daylight left," he said, "and I don't suppose it makes much difference where we stop to sleep tonight. Come on, then. Let's go take a look and see if you've found what you think you have."

Instead of staying with the faint trail than ran beside the Powder River, Jessie and Kelly cut across at an angle that would take them in a straight line to the twin buttes. With the heat of the day past, the haze that had shrouded the basin was beginning to dissipate. By the time they'd gotten halfway to their destination, the air had cleared enough to allow them to make out details of the buttes, and Jessie could see now that they were anything but the identical twins she'd taken them to be when looking at them from a more oblique angle.

Though the bases of both the buttes rose straight above a long slope that stretched away from them to the floor of the basin, the left butte towered high above its neighbor. Its face was sheer and rose in a symmetrical half circle from base to top. Its face was a medley of colored strips: light tan, ivory, deep buff, dark pink, dull orange. From the angle at which Jessie and Kelly were looking, the top of the higher butte seemed to be flat, and a dark layer of soil that overhung its top like a massive eyebrow indicated that the earth was thick enough to support the growth of grass and brush that they saw sprouting from the rim.

On their right, the lower butte had the same layered face, but it rose only two-thirds as high as its neighbor. This butte had a lopsided, rounded top, and it was evident at a glance that the top was free of soil, for it had no dark overhanging eyebrow. Its dome glowed a deep pink in the final rays of the setting sun and the slope of its face showed the varied layers of colors that marked the sides of its companion, layers formed countless thousands of years ago by dust sinking to the bottom of the prehistoric inland sea that had once covered the area.

"Do you think it's going to be too dark to see anything by the time we get up to the base of those buttes?" Jessie asked, looking at the sun now dipping below the horizon.

"They're farther away than they looked to be at first," Kelly said. "But even if it's dark when we get to them, we can stop at the base and make a dry camp. Then we'll get an early start in the morning and get an idea of how the land lays."

"If we hurry now, though, we can follow the tracks that herd of steers left," Jessie pointed out. "They ought to lead us to the place where they're bedded down."

"I'm not really sure we want to catch up with them tonight," Kelly said thoughtfully. "We don't know what the land's like beyond those buttes. I'm not even sure there's a trail leading between them."

"There must be!" Jessie protested. "After all, that's where I saw a whole herd of steers disappear. The hole has got to be between those two buttes, Sean!"

"Are you absolutely sure those cattle went between the buttes, Jessie?" Kelly asked. "I noticed that from where you were when we met up you couldn't see the bottom of the little one on the right."

"But I met you a half mile from where I saw the herd! And the place where I stopped was quite a way up the slope, too! I could see the base of that butte quite clearly, and I'm sure those steers went between them!"

"I'm not saying you're wrong, Jessie," her companion said quickly, "but I don't think we'd better get our hopes too high until we get a lot closer."

"Which won't take us long," Jessie told him. "Another ten minutes and we'll be starting up the slope. From there, it's not much more than a mile to the base of that first butte."

They rode on in silence until they reached a little ledge, an almost vertical rise that marked the beginning of the upslope that was crowned by the buttes. The earthen ledge was between five and six feet high and jutted up in a ragged half circle that was roughly parallel to the bases of the two buttes.

Kelly reined up in front of the abrupt rise and sat gazing past the ledge at the two massive stone formations. Jessie stopped when he did and they studied the upslope, the earth ledge, and the buttes for several moments before either of them spoke.

"I couldn't see this ledge from up above, Sean," Jessie said at last. "But it's certainly going to make our job of finding the trail of those steers a lot easier. All we have to do is ride along it until we find a break. A steer can't get up a bank as high as this one is."

"That's just what I was thinking," Kelly said. "Come on. We'll ride along it and look for the break."

Reining their horses to the right, they started riding along the face of the ledge. They'd covered almost a half-mile without seeing any change in its character. They'd come across only a few narrow wedges washed out by water from rains and melting snow. Jessie pointed ahead and exclaimed, "There it is, Sean! Just what we've been looking for, a break where cattle can be driven up to the buttes."

"And where cattle have been driven, too," Kelly said.

He pointed to the floor of the basin. Jessie looked in the direction he'd indicated and saw a number of faint streaks on its hard ground. They were so dim that in any light other than the low rays of the setting sun they would have been invisible from anywhere except the rim.

With the waning sunlight shining across them, the streaks looked like the outline of a gigantic arrowhead that had been traced in the basin's floor. They converged as they came closer to the break in the ledge that outlined the beginning of the basin, and from there they became a more visible trail that led to the gap between the buttes.

"My guess is that the hole is the name for that gap,"

Jessie said, pointing to the dark streak that separated the thrusting rock faces of the buttes.

"Of course," Kelly said. "And I've got to admit, it fits that opening." He glanced at the sky and went on, "We don't have much time left, Jessie. It'll be dark in a quarter hour or less. Do you want to put off going any farther until morning?"

"Not for a minute!" Jessie exclaimed. "We're too close to turn back now, Sean. We might as well take a look."

"Whatever you say," he said.

Moving as one, they wheeled their horses, rode over the broken area of the ledge, and mounted the slope, moving toward the gap. As they entered the slit between the buttes, they rode into dimness. It was not the darkness of night, but a deep twilight that obscured details of the ground and turned the faces of the buttes into dark, towering walls that seemed ready to close in on them.

"I wish we had more light," Jessie said after they'd ridden a dozen or so yards into the slit. "I'm sure that if we did we'd be able to see all sorts of tracks on the ground."

"You're probably right," Kelly said. "We'll have to wait until tomorrow for that, though."

As they rode deeper into the slit, the walls of the buttes curved, and the light was even dimmer between the sheer vertical walls. They could see even in the gloom that the passageway did not narrow. There was still room for Jessie and Kelly to ride abreast. They pushed on. Abruptly the passageway became straight. It extended for another hundred yards or more and ended in a low stone wall that rose above their heads for several feet, but showed no gap through which they could pass.

"It's not a hole after all!" Jessie exclaimed, her voice reflecting her disappointment. "Just a little blind canyon!"

"That what it looks like," Kelly replied soberly.

"But it's got to be more than just a blind canyon!" Jessie

went on. "All the cattle trails we saw leading in here certainly wouldn't have been there unless steers could go on through."

Jessie swung out of her saddle and started walking through the gloom to the end of the passageway. Kelly dismounted quickly and followed her. When he reached her, Jessie had stopped in front of the high stone wall that blocked the gap and was exploring its surface with her hands.

"It's solid stone, all right," she told him, her voice low and sober. "But I still don't believe it, Sean! There's got to be an opening here somewhere! There's too much evidence that this is a passageway to think of it being anything else!"

Kelly had started feeling the wall himself. He turned to Jessie, their faces ghostly blurs in the darkness that enveloped the narrow slit.

"I think you're right," he said. "But we're not going to find out anything about this place in the dark. The best thing we can do is to make camp close by and then come back and have a really good look in the morning."

"I don't suppose it'd be safe to camp right here," Jessie suggested. Then, before Kelly could reply, she went on, "Of course, it isn't! Let's go, then, Sean. I've been so wrapped up in finding our way into the hole that I hadn't realized until right this minute how hungry I am."

When they emerged from the deep blackness of the slit, the starlit night outside seemed bright. Kelly gestured toward the slope that stretched to the floor of the basin and said, "I don't see much point in going any farther away than we have to. Suppose we ride along the base of the butte and find a place to camp. It'll save us a ride in the morning."

"That'll suit me just fine," Jessie replied. "There's sure to be a level spot somewhere at the base, and I don't imagine there'll be anybody passing by to disturb us."

They rode along the base of the taller butte until they found a small area of level ground far enough from the opening so that they wouldn't be seen by anyone passing on the converging cattle trails. Jessie wasted no time in digging into her saddlebag and getting out the cheese and crackers left over from her lunch.

"Wouldn't you like some dried beef to go with that?" Kelly asked her. "There's plenty left in the rations bag and some boiled potatoes, too, if you'd rather have them than bread."

"Open the bag, then, and we'll sit down and eat together," she said as Kelly started untying the strings that held the canvas bag to his saddle. "I'll spread a blanket. It won't soften the ground any, but it'll be a little bit more comfortable."

She untied the strings that held her bedroll, and while Kelly opened the food bag, she spread the blanket on the hard, smooth ground a little way from the tethered horses. He put the bag at the edge of the blanket where both of them could reach it and began taking out the ration packets prepared by the cook at Fort Casper. Settling down, they started eating. Even cold beef and boiled potatoes tasted good after a long day in the saddle, and they ate hungrily. There was little conversation until their appetites were satisfied.

"You were as hungry as I was," Jessie said after they'd slacked off. "And I certainly feel a lot better now."

"I was hungry," Kelly told her. He started putting the packets of uneaten food back in the rations bag. "But we were so busy trying to find where that trail led that I didn't notice it."

"It was nothing but luck that I saw the trail," Jessie told him. "If I hadn't missed the place where Salt Creek flows into the Powder, I wouldn't've been high enough above the basin to see that herd."

"I have a feeling that you make your own luck, Jessie," Kelly said. "And I only wish I'd run into you a long time ago."

"When I was younger and more susceptible to the advances of young army officers?" Jessie asked, the smile that flitted over her face hidden by the darkness, but reflected in her voice.

"You have a way of reading a man's mind," Kelly replied. "I saw that when you were talking to the major."

"If I do, it was because I had a good teacher."

"Your father? I know mine always said he'd learned more from him than anyone he'd ever met."

"Alex taught me a great deal," Jessie said, her voice sober. Then, shrugging sad memories aside, she added, "But the teacher I really meant was a wise Japanese woman. Alex put me in her hands to teach me about men, among other things."

"And were her teachings really extensive?"

"Oh, yes."

"Do you ever practice what you learned?"

"Sometimes. When I feel that I'm with the right man at the right time."

"If I'm being too forward, I hope you'll forgive me," Kelly said. "But I don't think you could've missed noticing the way I look at you sometimes."

"I haven't, Sean."

"Is this the right place and the right time?"

"It's as good a place and time as we're likely to have," she told him, her voice inviting.

Kelly needed no further encouragement. He slid across the blanket and took her in his arms. Jessie's response to his kiss encouraged him to go further, and she felt his hands full on her breasts. When she made no move to push his hands away, Kelly fumbled for the buttons of her blouse and opened it.

Jessie shrugged the thin blouse off her shoulders, allowing the straps of her thin chemise to drop at the same time. Kelly bent his head to caress her firm breasts with his lips and the tip of his tongue, and Jessie arched her back at the sensations his warm mouth created when he found the firm tips and began to caress them with his lips and tongue.

"When you do that, you make me want to purr like a cat," she said softly.

"I can do better," he promised. "Right now my scope's a bit limited."

"We're too dressed for lovemaking," Jessie suggested.

"Yes, we are. It's time we changed that, I think," Kelly replied.

He released her and stood up. Jessie got out of her boots and took off her gunbelt, laying the holstered Colt on the corner of the blanket. Then she stood up, quickly discarded her skirt and underclothes, and stretched her arms above her head. Her satiny skin gleamed in the soft starlight, its white smoothness accentuated by the puckered rosettes of her uplifted breasts and the dark triangle between her thighs.

She glanced at Kelly. He was just stepping out of his balbriggans. His eyes fixed on her. She looked with approval at the jutting shaft that stood out from his loins. He turned to her, and she stepped closer to him, grasping his shaft and guiding it between her thighs.

Kelly's arms were already around her when Jessie raised hers to embrace him. He pulled her to him, and Jessie turned her face up. Kelly's tongue parted her lips and she welcomed it with hers. As they clung together, she began to rotate her hips, caressing his erection. She enhanced her pleasure by twisting her shoulders to rasp the wiry mat on his chest against the sensitive tips that stood out from her breasts. She closed her eyes to shut out any distraction, enjoying the sensations that were mounting in her quivering body. As they grew stronger and more urgent, she broke their kiss gently.

"I think it's time now," she whispered.

"So do I," Kelly said.

He lifted Jessie in his arms and held her off the ground. Locking her ankles around Kelly's thighs, she pulled him into her until his shaft was buried fully. For a moment, Jessie stayed motionless, savoring the sensation of being filled. Then she began moving her hips, slowly at first and then faster.

Kelly held her to him for several minutes while Jessie kept up the movements that were beginning to bring her pleasure. Then he grasped her closer and dropped to his knees without breaking their junction. He thrust fiercely for a few moments, and each time he did, Jessie lifted her hips to meet him. When her lover's breathing grew gusty, Jessie exercised all the strength in her calves and thighs to stop his thrusts and hold him still.

"Don't be impatient," she whispered. "The longer we wait, the more we'll please each other."

When Kelly responded to her soft request by thrusting deep and holding himself against her, Jessie unlocked her ankles and spread her thighs wide. She bent her knees to plant the soles of her feet flat on Kelly's thighs. Holding herself with one arm around Kelly's back, she reached down to grasp her ankles and pull them still higher—until her toes were touching his hips.

"Now!" she whispered. "Go as fast and deep as you can!"

Kelly thrust with vigor, and Jessie sighed as he continued his deep penetrations. She was mounting to a peak rapidly now, and her lover was keeping pace with her. She started trembling, but held to her control until Kelly cried out and lunged forward with a final thrust. Then Jessie joined him in an explosive climax that seemed to ripple through them forever before their trembling bodies grew still and they lay quietly entwined.

They lay silent for a long while until their panting subsided. Then Kelly whispered, "You're a tremendous woman, Jessie. I hope you feel as good as I do now."

"Oh, I do," she assured him. "Let's sleep a little while now, but not too long. Dawn will be here much too soon, and I don't want to waste a minute of our first night together."

★

Chapter 10

"I'm not sure this is the wisest move we can make," Kelly said as he and Jessie reined their horses into the narrow passage between the twin buttes.

"Why?" Jessie inquired. "We decided yesterday that we'd come back as soon as there was enough light to see by."

"I know we did. But even if the place seems deserted now, you saw cattle being trailed through here yesterday, and for all we know there might be another herd coming in today."

"If there was another herd on the way, we'd have seen it coming while we were crossing the basin," Jessie told him.

"Suppose it was still out of sight when we could see the basin?" he asked.

Jessie smiled and shook her head. She said, "Unless you've been on a cattle drive, you don't realize how slowly a herd moves."

"That's an experience I've never had," he said. "But do

you mean that even if there was a herd close enough for us to see, it still couldn't get here while we're in the passage?"

"Exactly," Jessie stated. "A herd of cattle moves like a snail."

"I'm sure you've been on enough cattle drives to know," Kelly said, "so I won't worry about one being on the way."

When the first hint of daybreak had been visible on the eastern horizon, Jessie and Kelly had started for the cut between the buttes. Though they'd slept only intermittently between their bouts of furious lovemaking, both of them felt fresh. The hint of daybreak had turned into dawn while they were riding to the cleft in the buttes, and by the time they reached it, the rim of the rising sun was flooding the sky with light. As they advanced along the curving passage between the towering stone walls, the light trickling into the cleft grew steadily brighter.

Ahead of them, the stone barrier that had baffled them the evening before came into sight. It still looked formidable, but now they could see that its face was not as forbidding as it had seemed in the darkness of the previous evening. What had then appeared to be a solid barrier now showed itself for what it was, a lopsided cleft of bedrock strewn with small boulders that had rolled down and lay scattered in the notch. Even where the boulders were piled up, they could see daylight through the cracks between them.

"That doesn't look at all like it did yesterday evening," Jessie said as they reined in. "With all those cracks showing, you can see that it's not a solid wall."

"I see something else, too," Kelly told her. "Look at the way that line of little boulders strings down the side of the butte. Does that look natural to you?"

Jessie studied the line of stones that stood on a ledge slanting down the wall of the butte to the bottom of the cleft. Some were almost as big as a man's torso, but most of them were smaller. After she'd run her eyes over the stones for a moment, she shook her head.

"It's not natural, Sean. We'd have seen yesterday evening that it wasn't if there'd been enough light. Somebody's put those stones there."

"That ledge is wider than it looks from down here, too," he said. Swinging out of his saddle, he walked along the wall toward the mouth of the passage. In a moment he called, "Come back here, Jessie! I think I've found something else that's real interesting."

Dismounting, Jessie walked back to join him. Kelly was standing beside a line of a dozen or so flat stones that angled down from the wall of the butte to a narrow ledge that slanted upward. He pointed to the area covered by the stones.

"Does that look natural to you, Jessie?" he asked.

After she'd examined them for a moment, Jessie shook her head and said, "No. They're not at all like any of the other stones around here. They look like they belong somewhere else."

"That's what struck me, too," Kelly said.

He stepped over to a stone and began prying at its side. After a moment he lifted the stone and stepped back. On the bottom of the area the stone had hidden, between the bottom of the passage and the almost vertical side of the butte, there was a well-defined trail, and near its center the hoofprint of a horse was impressed in a thin layer of loose dirt.

Jessie glanced up the wall of the passage. Where the line of flat, slanting stones ended, she could now see a narrow ledge, the rocks along its edge keeping it hidden from someone looking up the wall of the butte from below.

"Those rocks up there are just a border!" she exclaimed. "Sean, this is a trail that goes up to that notch! And I'll bet those boulders that're piled up in the notch are camouflage, too, just like the stones along this ledge! Looking up at them from below, you can't see this ledge at all!"

"I'm inclined to think you're right," Kelly said and nodded.

"Then we've found it!" Jessie said. "We've found the secret of the hole!"

"It won't take us long to make sure," Kelly said.

He began lifting away the thin flat stones that leaned above the one he'd already removed. They were longer than the first, and he needed to wrestle away only two of them to uncover the beginning of a ledge that was wide enough to allow a horse or a steer to walk up it.

"This is the trail into the hole, all right," Jessie told him confidently. "It wouldn't be any trick at all to haze steers up that ledge. It'd take time because the ledge is narrow, but once the steers were out of sight in the passage between the buttes, that wouldn't matter."

"Of course not," Kelly said. "They wouldn't have to worry about how long it took. Why, they could haze the steers up the ledge in single file if they wanted to."

"And that's not a very hard job for a top cowhand," Jessie commented thoughtfully. She stepped onto the area Kelly had uncovered and looked up it. Turning back to him, she went on, "Let's leave our horses here and walk to the top, Sean. I want to see what sort of place the hole leads to."

"It's daylight now, Jessie!" Kelly protested. "If you saw a herd being driven in here yesterday, that must mean there are people somewhere close."

"They won't see me if I'm careful," she said confidently.

"You mean they won't see us," Kelly told her. "Because if you're going through the hole, I'm going with you!"

Kelly's emphatic tone told Jessie that protesting would

be futile. She nodded and said, "We'll tether the horses and go together. And it shouldn't be too much of a risk if we're careful."

After seeing to the horses, Jessie and Kelly started up the ledge. Jessie carried her Winchester, Kelly his Ballard carbine. The ledge proved surprisingly easy to mount. Its slope was gentle and the boulders that camouflaged it kept those ascending it from getting dangerously near the rim.

As they moved up the sloping trail, the ledge widened. At the point where it entered the notch between the two buttes, the well-used path would easily have accommodated four people walking abreast. They reached the notch and started walking up the low embankment beyond it. Moving slowly now and with greater caution, they advanced until they got their first view of the terrain that stretched out ahead of them. Then they stopped and gazed with growing surprise at what they saw.

In front of them lay a broad, oval-shaped valley where green grass rippled in a gentle breeze. A shallow curving crease cut through the center and ended at a high escarpment three or four miles distant. The rock formation was as sheer as a manmade wall, and even from a distance, they could see it was a barrier that sealed the opposite end of the valley very effectively.

Looking along the valley floor, they got an occasional glimpse of the sun's rays reflected from the rippling surface of a small creek. There were a half dozen cabins in the valley; they were scattered in no apparent pattern. Only two of the structures were large; the rest were cabins that at best could have had no more than two rooms. Low chimneys made from lengths of stovepipe rose above the gabled roofs of the cabins. They saw a man standing, a rifle held in the crook of his arm.

Two herds of cattle were visible; they were grazing on the tall grass. One was isolated at the far end of the shallow valley; the other herd was near its center. Riders were slowly circling the larger herd. A half dozen horses and a mule wandered aimlessly along the creek, grazing as they moved.

"Why, this is a rustler's paradise!" Jessie exclaimed.

"Rustlers, smugglers, killers, any kind of outlaw who might need a safe place to hide out," Kelly stated. "I wouldn't be surprised to find some army deserters in one of those cabins."

"What surprises me is how Sang Thompson manages to keep the location of this place a secret," Jessie said. "Just look at it! Houses, cattle, horses! It's like a town, Sean."

"It is, at that," Kelly said. "But we managed to find it. It can't be too hard for people looking for a safe hideaway to learn about it, and those who're on the wrong side of the law learn how to keep secrets."

"Alex used to say that a secret shared by more than two people stops being a secret." Jessie smiled.

"What's important is that we've found this place," Kelly said. "But now we've come to the hard part, Jessie."

"Finding Ki and getting him out?"

"That's what I'm thinking about, yes."

"Finding him isn't any problem, Sean. We've already done that. I'm sure that the man in front of the cabin over there is standing guard and that Ki's inside."

"And I'm sure you're right. I've been thinking the same thing. That reduces our problem to getting him out, to say nothing of getting ourselves out."

"We can do it if we work fast," Jessie said confidently. "I think our best move is to leave now before anybody sees us. Then we'll come back around sundown, and as soon as it's dark enough, we shouldn't have much trouble getting to that cabin. And after we've gotten Ki free, we'll worry about getting out."

. . .

Dusk was graying the sky when Jessie and Sean returned to the hole. They'd been careful to replace the slabs that hid the beginning of the trail into the hidden valley. Jessie had put a pebble on each slab to give them a warning that someone had entered or left while they were gone, and the markers were undisturbed. Working quickly, they removed the slabs and started up the ledge to the outlaw haven.

"We're going to get there at just about the right time," Jessie said, looking at the slit of sky that outlined where the twin buttes converged.

Kelly's eyes followed Jessie's upward glance. A few pale stars were showing and the sky was darkening from gray to the deep blue of night.

"It'll be dark in another ten minutes," he stated.

They reached the edge of the hidden valley. The yellow glow of lamplight already showed in the windows of the cabins, and from the far end of the valley, the occasional moan of a steer broke the otherwise silent air. Jessie had marked in her mind the location of the cabin where she was sure Ki had been placed. The shadowy figure of a man moving in front of it told her that there was still a guard on duty.

"If all the guesswork we've done is anywhere near right, I ought to be able to get to the cabin where they're holding Ki and put the guard out of commission without making any noise or attracting attention," she told Kelly. "With a little bit of luck, we'll have Ki free and be gone before anybody knows we've even been here."

"I still think I ought to be the one to go to that cabin and get him out," Kelly said. "If somebody should get suspicious and raise an alarm—"

Jessie broke in. "No, Sean. We've settled that. Ki will recognize my voice and know what to do when he hears it. And if there's trouble, we've met it together before. I can take care of myself; you don't have to worry about me."

"Just the same, I feel sort of silly——"

"Don't," Jessie broke in on him for the second time. "It's just as important for us to get out as it is to get in. We settled all that when we made our plans."

"I suppose so," Kelly replied, his voice showing that he was still reluctant. "But be careful."

"Of course. Now, it's dark enough for me to be able to move without attracting attention." She handed Kelly her Winchester. "This is just excess baggage right now. My Colt is all I'll need."

"What about Ki? Can't he use it?"

"He can, but he doesn't need it. Ki fights in his own way. And if I'm lucky, I won't need my Colt. Look for us in about a half hour, Sean."

"Go on, then," Kelly told Jessie, pulling her to him for a quick kiss. "I'll be watching for you."

Jessie slipped away, following the trail to the valley floor instead of circling over the rocks at its edge. She stepped across the creek and angled toward the first of the cabins. The grass brushed her legs as she made her way toward the widely spaced buildings.

Keeping well away from the splash of light that poured from an unshaded window, Jessie circled the cabin in order to get behind it. She glanced inside as she passed the window. Three men sat at a table. They were eating. Jessie did not stop to look at them, but made for the darkness behind the cabin. She moved through it and past the two larger buildings and a small cabin beyond them to the one where she was sure Ki was being held.

By the time Jessie reached the cabin where Ki was being held, her eyes had regained the night vision lost when she looked into the lighted cabin. Jessie could see the sentry clearly again, a black form pacing slowly back and forth in front of the cabin, softly whistling a tune. She could make out the barrel of the rifle that he carried, its butt in his armpit and its muzzle pointed toward the ground. His hat stood out against the starlit sky. Jessie stopped and hunkered down in the grass while she silently counted seconds to time his progress from one side of the cabin to the other.

After she was sure she'd be able to reach her goal while the cabin shielded her from his eyes, Jessie waited until the man in front had turned and started away from her. Taking the longest steps she could manage while still moving silently, she reached the cabin's corner several seconds before the sentry returned.

By now the night had settled in fully, and even though Jessie's eyes had adjusted to the blackness, her vision was very limited. She began feeling her way along the wall of the little shack, hoping to find a window or door that would allow her to enter the cabin silently and unseen.

Her fingers told her that the window on the side where she started had been covered with boards. When she felt her way along the rear wall, she discovered that the shack had no back door. Having found the window in one side boarded, she assumed that if there were a similar one on the opposite side, it would also have been boarded.

There was only one decision to make, and Jessie made it without delay. She groped her way to the front corner of the cabin and drew her Colt. When the sentry's shadowy figure reached the corner again, Jessie groaned loudly.

She saw the guard stop instantly. With the smoothly automatic movements of an experienced gunman, he leveled the gun while he swiveled his head trying to find the source of the sound.

Dropping to the ground, Jessie groaned again. The sentry's head turned at once, and Jessie could tell that he'd seen her, for he took a step toward her. As he moved, he shifted the muzzle of the rifle to cover her.

For the third time, Jessie groaned. The guard was within

a step of her now. He stopped, bending forward as he peered through the darkness at her prone form.

"Who the hell are you?" he asked.

"Help me," Jessie moaned.

"Damned if you ain't a woman!" the sentry exclaimed as he bent still lower. "Who are you and what're you doing here?"

At that point Jessie struck. Grabbing the barrel of the man's rifle, she jerked it forward, throwing the sentry off balance. As he lurched ahead still bent double, Jessie swung her Colt like a club. The barrel of the heavy revolver landed with a crushing *thud* on the man's head. His hat crumpled as Jessie's blow went home. He grunted explosively and the rifle dropped to the ground as he toppled forward across its stock and lay still.

After hurrying to the door, Jessie tried its knob, even though she was sure it would be locked. It was. She returned to the unconscious guard and searched the pockets of his trousers, found no key, then dipped her fingers into the lower pockets of his vest, and felt the key in the second pocket she tried. After rushing back to the door, she put the key into the lock and swung the door open. The interior of the cabin was deep black. Jessie could see nothing.

"Ki?" she called, her voice only a little above a whisper.

"Over here, Jessie. To your left and against the wall."

As Jessie slowly moved forward, Ki went on, "You'll need a knife. My hands and feet are both tied, and I don't imagine we've got very much time to waste."

"None at all," Jessie told him. "And I don't have a knife. But the sentry won't bother us. He'll stay unconscious long enough for me to untie you."

Her shin touched a barrier as she was speaking. She bent, ran her fingers down Ki's arm to his wrists, and felt the rope that bound them.

116

"It's just a tie," he said. "A tight one, though. But if you can find the loose end—"

Jessie's fingers had located the knot by now. It was the same one used by cowhands when securing the hooves of a roped steer. The knot was one that could be tied quickly and tightly, but could be untied with equal speed by a single pull of its dangling end. Jessie found the end and yanked hard and the twists around Ki's wrists loosened.

"You'll have to untie my feet, too," he said. "I almost got free when they were carrying me away from the train, and since then, they've kept me tied except when I ate. My hands are going to be numb until I work with them a few minutes."

"Can you walk?" Jessie asked, pulling the rope that bound Ki's ankles.

"Well enough. I'll be clumsy at first," Ki replied as he sat up on the cot. "But that'll wear off soon."

"We'd better go," she told him, groping for his hand to help him stand up.

A shot sounded outside the cabin; then the figure of the guard blotted out the rectangle of lesser dimness that marked the door. His rifle cracked again. The slug made a soft plop as it tore into the thin mattress of the bed near where Ki had been lying.

Jessie's Colt barked before the guard could fire again. The sentry toppled forward and lay still on the cabin floor.

Jessie and Ki started for the door of the cabin. Before they reached it, they heard shouts from outside and the sound of slamming doors. With the quickness of men used to living on danger's edge, the outlaws were reacting to the threat to their hide-out.

Chapter 11

"Quick!" Jessie said. "This cabin's going to be like an anthill in a few minutes!"

"Behind the cabin?" Ki asked as he started for the door.

"It's the only place we can reach before they get here," Jessie said. "And it'll be the first place they'll look for us, too."

"It'll take them a few minutes to sort things out and get organized," Ki told her as they got outside and started for the back of the shack.

Jessie glanced around as she moved. Dark forms were hurrying toward the cabin. In two or three of the other dwellings lights were glowing. When they stopped behind the shack, they could see nothing except the glow of lighted windows reflected on the ground. Their ears told them what was happening, and a sudden glow that spread around the front of the cabin told them that someone had lighted a lamp or lantern.

"Who done the shooting?" one of the men there asked.

"Damned if I know," another answered. "Me and Tobe was asleep when it wakened us up. We looked out and seen some lamps lighting up and then a lantern heading this way. That's all I know."

"You seen my lantern," a fresh voice said. "I had a bellyache and couldn't go to sleep. There were two shots, a rifle and a handgun. I could tell they come from up this way. Blackie and Charley woke up and we come to see what it was all about."

"Looks like Flatnose got off the first shot," still another announced. "He's still got hold of his rifle. But the other one come from a pistol."

"That'd be the one that got him," the first voice said.

"There's outsiders in the hole, then," the second man broke in. "We better make a sweep and see if we can grab 'em."

"Wait'll everybody's here, Goose," said the man who'd been the first to speak. "Don't let's go off half-cocked. Dark as it is, one of us might take a wrong bullet."

Listening to the outlaws, Ki said, "We've got to move before they start looking for us, Jessie. And all I've seen up here is the inside of this cabin. They blindfolded me before we got here. But you must know the lay of the land."

"Well enough to get us out if we can shake off those men in front," she told him. "And well enough to know there's no place to hide."

"There's always a place to hide!" Ki insisted. "We—"

Jessie broke in. "Maybe there is, Ki. At the upper end of the valley, there's a little herd of steers. In the dark they won't be feisty enough to bother us, and we can dodge along the backs of the cabins to get to them."

"Close to the entrance?"

"No. On the far side of the valley from it. But the path

in is the path out, so that's the first place the outlaws will look. Maybe they'll even set a guard there. But they'll be spread pretty thin when they start hunting us, and we'll find a way to slip past them in the dark."

Fresh voices were coming from the group in front of the cabin, and as much as Jessie would have liked to stay and listen for more names, she knew that she and Ki would have little chance of escaping unless they got out of the valley at once.

"Let's move before they get their search organized, Ki," she suggested. "Sean Kelly's waiting at the trail that leads out, but I'm not too worried about him. He's got my rifle as well as his own, and he's used to fighting."

"I won't waste time asking you who he is, Jessie," Ki said as Jessie started toward the next cabin. "Go ahead, I'll keep up. My legs have some feeling back in them now."

Both Jessie and Ki knew the tricks of evading enemies. Jessie did not run. She moved at a slow walk, bending as far forward as she dared without losing her balance. Ki could bend lower and move faster at that stance than she could, and though his muscles still suffered from the long days when he'd been lying with his legs lashed together, he had no trouble keeping up.

Before the outlaws had gotten their pursuit organized, she and Ki had covered the wide open space between the cabin that had been his prison and the next cabin and were able then to straighten up and run to the large buildings, which gave them better cover.

They moved unhesitatingly past the remaining small cabins and pushed on through the darkness until they could hear the occasional noises that came from the cattle herd ahead of them. They slowed their pace now and looked back. The glow of bobbing lanterns broke the darkness around the cabins and, as they watched, the pinpoints of yellow light spread into a line that stretched almost completely across the floor of the little valley and then started moving slowly toward them.

"They didn't waste much time in getting their search organized," Ki commented. "We'll have to break through that line somehow in order to get back to where you said your friend is waiting."

"It won't be too hard," Jessie said. "Head toward that high cliff that rises along the wall over there."

"Planning to climb it to get away?" Ki asked.

"Of course. It's got plenty of cracks that run from the base to the top," Jessie told him. "Now that we've got a minute to talk, I'd better tell you about Sean Kelly. He's a captain stationed at Fort Casper who volunteered to come help me find this place."

"But he didn't come into the hole with you?"

"I wouldn't let him. All the U.S. Army knows is how to fight in a formation."

"Well, you're right about that. We'll have horses to get away on, then?" Ki asked.

"Of course. Two, but you and I have ridden double before."

"Then we still want to get across the valley to the cliff."

"Yes, of course. But we'll be able to get away from these outlaws once we get to where Sean's waiting with the horses."

As they'd drawn closer to the steers, the moans of the cattle had grown louder. Now they could see the vague forms of the animals ahead.

"We'd better start across to the cliff right now," Ki suggested, "before those lights get too close to us."

"Yes," Jessie said. "We'll be—"

A rifle barked a few yards ahead of them and a slug whistled angrily only inches from Jessie's head. She and Ki dropped to the ground before the rifleman could get off another shot, and his second bullet sang through the air well above them.

"All right, you two!" a rasping voice called. "I got both of you spotted against them lights. On your feet now and git your hands high while you're standing up!"

"Do what he says, Ki," Jessie whispered. "We'll get close enough to handle him before the others can see us."

Keeping his voice as low as Jessie's, Ki replied, "About two steps is all I need. Be ready."

Keeping their hands high, Jessie and Ki slowly stood up. They could see the man who held the rifle on them now, and both of them realized that he must have caught sight of them silhouetted in the light of the lanterns.

"Didn't figure there'd be anybody watching the herd, did you?" the man holding the rifle asked gloatingly as they moved toward him. "Hell, I been watching you since you got out from behind them shanties. Now, stop edging up on me! You git another inch closer and I'll cut you down!"

"We've got enough sense to know when we're beaten," Jessie said to divert the outlaw's attention from Ki.

"A woman, by God!" the man said. He leaned forward and peered at Jessie. "Now I'd like to know just what—"

Whatever the man wanted to know, it was lost forever. In the moment when his attention was drawn to Jessie, Ki launched himself in an attack.

Before the outlaw could swing his rifle up, Ki was sailing through the air, and when his leap brought him close enough to the guard, he lashed out with a kick that whirled him in midair. His heel crashed into the gunman's head, landing on the soft complex of bones above the man's ear and just in front of it.

With his dying reflex, the man tightened his finger on the trigger of his rifle. The bullet plowed into the ground. He was dead before he could get off another shot, killed by

123

the shards of bone Ki's kick had driven into his brain. He started crumpling to the ground, the rifle falling from his hands as he collapsed.

Ki's momentum had carried him a yard past the point where the man had fallen. As he hit the ground, he rolled to his feet in one fluid move and started back toward Jessie.

"We've got to hurry, Ki!" she said. She picked up the dead man's rifle and tossed it to Ki. "Those shots have started the others running!"

"That herder had to have a horse, Jessie!" Ki said. "And it's got to be close! We'll have a better chance to get away if we're on horseback."

Jessie looked back toward the cabins. From the erratic bobbing of the lanterns the outlaws carried, she could tell that the shot fired by the herder had started them running.

"We'll have to find it fast!" she exclaimed.

Jessie folded her fingers and whistled the shrill sound commonly used on the range to summon a standing horse. Over the voices of the approaching outlaw gang, she heard a nicker from the darkness ahead. Ki heard it, too, and was already moving in the direction of the sound. As Jessie started to follow him, she whistled again, and again the horse nickered from the darkness.

"I've located it, Jessie!" Ki called over his shoulder. "Hurry up! It'll carry us double for the little distance we need to cover!"

Following the sound of Ki's voice, Jessie ran toward him. He was only a dozen paces away, holding the horse by its dangling reins.

"You get in the saddle," he told Jessie. "I'll ride the crupper and hold them off!"

When the outlaws had started running after hearing the shot, the line they'd formed originally had broken. They were running ahead now in a loose formation, all of them heading for the point where they'd seen the muzzle flashes.

When Jessie saw the lights drawing together, she said over her shoulder to Ki, "Don't use that rifle yet. They can't see much beyond those lanterns. I'm going to break them up!"

Less than a hundred yards separated Jessie and Ki from the advancing outlaws. They'd drawn closer together now, the lanterns they carried outlining them clearly. Jessie pounded the horse's flanks with her heels, and the animal put on a burst of speed. It swung its head as it got closer to the moving lights, but Jessie's hands were gripping the reins firmly.

The galloping horse hit the clustered outlaws. Some of them had tried to scatter. The horse dashed through the outlaws at full tilt, its weight and speed sending most of them sprawling to the ground.

Only a few had enough presence of mind to fire at Jessie and Ki as the horse broke through the clustered men. The shots were all wild, for they had no time to aim before triggering their weapons. Jessie and Ki got a fleeting impression of some moving figures and angry faces before the speeding horse carried them through their antagonists and into the darkness beyond.

Jessie glanced back over her shoulder as the yells of the outlaws began dying away. She saw a scene of wild confusion. Some of the men who'd felt themselves falling had grabbed at the others. Several lanterns had flown from the hands of the men carrying them. The lanterns had been dashed to the ground, their glass chimneys breaking and kerosene spilling and igniting when it flowed over the burning wicks. The grass was too green to burn, but in spots where the kerosene puddled, it had burst into flame, and low-burning blazes flickered in several places. A few of the men who'd gotten a kerosene shower were beating at their flaming clothing, trying to extinguish the fire.

"I don't think we'll have to worry about them for a while," Jessie said over her shoulder to Ki.

"They'll be busy long enough for us to get a good start on them," Ki stated. "Now all we've got to do is find your friend and get out of here before those fellows can get organized to follow us."

"I think they'll be too smart to try following us in the dark, Ki," Jessie replied. "And once we're out of the hole, they won't know which way we'll be headed."

Free from harassment for the moment, Jessie reined their captured horse toward the sheer wall of the canyon. They rode beside it until Sean Kelly heard the animal's hoofbeats and hailed them.

"Jessie! Over here! And I hope you've got your friend with you!"

"I have," she replied as she and Ki drew to a halt beside him. "Even though you can't see one another very clearly, Ki, this is Captain Sean Kelly. Sean, I've told you about Ki, my good friend."

"Glad to meet you, Ki," Kelly said as he turned to lead the way down the ledge to the floor of the basin. "We'll get better acquainted as soon as we're far enough from here to stop and shake hands."

"Of course," Ki replied. "But I will give you my thanks now for helping Jessie."

"You'll have plenty of time to talk later," Jessie broke in. "Those outlaws are going to be after us like a pack of hungry wolves, and we've got to get away from them while it's still dark. They won't show us any mercy if they catch us. We're ahead of them now, so let's put all the distance we can between us and the hole."

"Let me make sure I understand you, Major Halloran," Jessie said, suppressing her anger and choosing her words carefully. "You refuse to send a platoon of your men to clear out that nest of rustlers and robbers?"

"That's correct, Miss Starbuck," Halloran replied. "And I intend to stand on my decision no matter what you do. If you want to carry out the threat you made when you came here before and send a message to President Hayes, I'll make our army telegraph line available."

"You may never have another chance like this—to catch them when they're still disorganized and confused," she pointed out.

"I won't argue that point with you," Halloran said stiffly. "But I still feel that an outlaw hide-out is a matter for civilian officials to handle."

"Major, you know quite well that what you call the civilian officials in this part of the Wyoming Territory means one marshal in Casper," Jessie said. "He'd be facing fifteen or twenty men in that hide-out!"

"Then let him form a posse," the major told her.

"I suggested that to him before coming out here," Jessie replied. "He's tried to get a posse up before in order to find the hole and wipe out that nest of crooks, but the good citizens of Casper aren't interested because so far the outlaws haven't bothered the town."

"And the army isn't interested," Halloran said. "My men are here to keep the redskins from making trouble. Just for your information, Miss Starbuck, I've consulted by telegraph with the Chief of Staff in Washington. If you bring the President into this, my superior officers are prepared to support my position that the army's function is to protect the civilian population from Indian forays."

Jessie stood up. "Very well," she said. "I'm not going to press you because, since it's no longer a secret, I'm not sure there'd be any outlaws left at the hole by now. I'm equally sure that there will be again in a few years, but that's neither your problem nor mine. Good day."

Ki had been waiting outside the headquarters building. He read Jessie's face and said, "I see the major turned you down, Jessie."

"Yes. But when I said good-bye to Sean Kelly, he warned me that's what would happen, so I'm not really surprised."

"It may be just as well that the major turned you down," Ki went on. "We haven't had a chance until now to talk privately, and I didn't want to say anything in front of your friend the captain."

"Say anything about what?"

"Things that I overheard while the outlaws were holding me prisoner—things that I know will be very interesting to you."

"If they're things Don Carter ought to know about, maybe you'd better wait, Ki."

Ki shook his head. "I don't think they're matters Don ought to know, Jessie. You can tell him as much as you want to later, of course, but right now I believe you should know the whole story yourself."

"Go ahead, then," Jessie said. "It'll take us a while to get back to Casper."

"You know how people are about us Orientals," Ki began. "It seems that everyone still seems to think that we can't understand English just because our eyes aren't like theirs."

Jessie nodded. "So the outlaws did a lot of talking just as though you weren't there?"

"Much more than I'd expected them to say, especially on the way to the hole from where they captured me. I know they didn't understand what they gave away because they still don't know anything about the cartel."

"Sometimes I think we don't know much, but go ahead."

"Your guess about grabbing land was correct, Jessie. The cartel wants all the Wyoming land it can get, especially if it's located where they'll get control of headwaters."

"But I was just reading what Alex had jotted down, Ki!"

"Your father was wiser than both of us," Ki replied. "But we've always known that. The important thing is that the cartel is trying to spread its hold over the West. Of course, you'd guessed that from Alex's notes. But there's something else equally important, Jessie."

"Go on." She frowned when Ki paused. "What's more important than knowing their plans?"

"Knowing for certain the name of the man who's responsible for carrying them out," Ki told her, "the chief cartel boss in this part of the West."

"And you learned it?"

"I'm sure I have," Ki said soberly. "He's a member of the British branch of the cartel. His name's Lord Sidney Harrington. He lives in Colorado just below the Wyoming border at Fort Collins. He has a big ranch there."

"These men who captured you knew all that?" Jessie asked incredulously.

"They knew it without knowing what they knew, Jessie. Lord Sidney had hired those outlaws to capture you! They were getting ready to go to Casper and take you prisoner, but you spoiled their plans by hitting them first."

Jessie rode on without speaking for a moment. Then she said, "I think we'd better not plan to go back to the Circle Star just yet, Ki. We'll start south as soon as we can, but we'll stop off for a while somewhere close to that ranch you just mentioned. I intend to find out exactly what is going on, and then you and I will do whatever we have to do to stop them!"

Chapter 12

"That must be Fort Collins ahead," Jessie said to Ki as they turned their horses down the long incline toward the little cluster of houses in the wide, shallow valley below them. "I'm glad to see it because it's been a long ride and I'm getting hungry."

"I'm still hungry from the hole," Ki said. "The outlaws only fed me once a day and not very much."

Jessie was still looking around. She said, "You know, Ki, as much as I detest the cartel I can almost sympathize with it for wanting this country. It's so beautiful. We don't have scenery like this around the Circle Star. Look at that grass on the range between here and town."

The road along which they were riding stretched eastward to a horizon almost as limitless as that of the Texas prairies. Behind them, the Rockies rose in rugged escarpments that in the distance became jutting peaks that seemed to touch the cloudless sky. The deep green of the cedars and pines that cloaked the flanks of the high peaks contrasted sharply with the lighter hue of the grasses that covered the flatland that shelved from the mountains before dimpling into the shallow valley into which they were now riding.

"It's as fine country for cattle as you'll see anywhere," Ki said. "I remember hearing your father say that years ago when he was trying to decide whether he wanted to buy the land for his ranch here in northern Colorado or in Texas."

"I was at school in the East when he was planning the Circle Star. What made him decide on Texas?"

"It was more isolated, and that was the whole idea of the ranch—to give him a place where he could find some solitude, time to think and plan."

"Well, as much as I love the open prairie, I enjoy seeing mountains on the horizon, too," Jessie said. "I suppose that's why Colorado has so much appeal for the Englishmen who bought ranches here. Living in that foggy, rainy country, they must've wanted to be where the sun shines and where there are wide horizons."

"Not all of them had such pure motives, Jessie," Ki reminded her. "From what I overheard, I'm sure that Lord Harrington came here on orders from the cartel. Of course, the outlaws didn't know who the orders came from, but I got the impression that it didn't take them long to figure out that Harrington was getting his instructions from somebody else and was just passing on the orders to them."

"I'm not forgetting that he's a cartel hireling, Ki," Jessie told him. "The main reason we're going to visit him is to see if we can't get some leads that will help us uncover his secret bosses."

"You've got a plan?"

"Certainly, I have! We may have to change it, but a man in Harrington's position with the cartel must get written orders from time to time. I'm sure he doesn't think we suspect him, so we should be able to get him to invite us in while I ask him to withdraw his offer for that land I arranged for Don Carter to buy. Once we're inside, it shouldn't be too hard to figure out where he keeps important papers."

"Of course," Ki said. "Then we'll know exactly where to look when we come back and examine them."

"Something like that," Jessie said. "This is the first chance we've had in quite a while to attack the cartel instead of waiting for them to attack us. I don't want to miss it, Ki."

They were approaching the town now. A little stream ran along its eastern edge. The valley fell away beyond its banks in an expanse of lush land that extended to the horizon. There were, Jessie thought, surprisingly few cattle, only a half dozen scattered herds. The cattle were not bunched, but spread out and moving slowly as they grazed. In the distance, too far for the naked eye to pick out details, there were a few scattered houses that stood apart from barns and small corrals.

Splashing across the narrow, shallow river that curved around the town, Jessie and Ki rode along a street flanked by small stores mixed with houses. The small shops gave way to a row of yellow brick buildings that housed a hotel and its restaurant, a dry goods emporium, a general store, and a number of saloons.

"Suppose we eat at the hotel, Ki," Jessie suggested. "And after we've eaten, we might as well register. They can tell us where Lord Harrington's ranch is located, and unless it's very close, I'd just as soon stop now and go out there tomorrow."

"Whatever you say." Ki nodded. "Lord Harrington's not expecting us, and a few hours aren't going to make any difference."

After a surprisingly good meal, Jessie and Ki stopped at the registration desk. Jessie asked the clerk, "How far is Lord Harrington's ranch from town?"

"About four miles to the east," he replied. "But if you came to see him, I'm afraid you're going to be disappointed. He died just over a week ago."

"Died?" Jessie asked. Her voice showed her consternation.

"Quite unexpected, ma'am, from what I've heard," the clerk stated. "The old bas—" He stopped quickly and went on. "The old fellow seemed in good health when I saw him just a few days before. He had a bunch of men in here for dinner, and he looked healthy enough then. You're a friend of his, I suppose."

"Not exactly," Jessie said. "I wanted to discuss a business matter with him."

"I imagine his widow would talk to you," the clerk said. "She's still at the ranch."

Jessie turned to Ki and raised her eyebrows questioningly. He nodded and she turned back to the clerk. "If you'll tell us how to get to the ranch, we'll go out there now. We'll register when we come back to town."

"His place isn't hard to find," the man told her. "Just take the first left you come to after you cross the river at the southern edge of town. You'll know it when you see it. It's a large stone"—he stopped as though trying to think of the proper word and then went on—"a large stone house standing quite a bit back and north of the road."

Both Jessie and Ki were thoughtfully silent as they rode out of town, following the hotel clerk's directions. As their horses moved along the narrow road, Jessie said, "I've been trying to figure out what effect Lord Harrington's death might have on the situation here. I expect you have, too."

"Of course," Ki replied. "Knowing the cartel's pattern, we can be sure they've got someone ready to replace Lord Harrington, but there'll be some floundering around before things settle down."

"Which might make our job easier, Ki," Jessie said.

"Yes," Ki said. "Until their new man learns what's involved in carrying out their plans, they'll be vulnerable."

Jessie nodded and said, "Harrington's probably been their key man in this area for a long time."

"I concur with your opinion," Ki said.

"I'm sure he had a safe or some sort of secure hiding place for his cartel papers. Just think how useful they could be to us!" Jessie said. "It'd be worth any amount of time and risk to get our hands on them."

"We'll have to—" Ki began to speak, but then stopped and pointed ahead. "What is that place on the hill there, Jessie? It looks like one of the old castles that I saw when I was with Alex in Europe."

Jessie's eyes widened as she looked in the direction Ki was pointing to. On the crest of a low hill and a short distance off the road, the turrets and battlements of a towering stone structure jutted above the horizon, outlined against the clear sky. In the gentle breeze, banners and pennants fluttered from all the turrets and at half-mast on a flagpole above the tallest of them, the British Union Jack rippled against the sky.

A carefully trimmed lawn stretched a hundred yards from the structure on all sides. Beyond the grassy area, there were buildings, stables, barns, and sheds, as well as several small dwellings. On the rolling hills that were visible past the imposing main building and the cluster of smaller ones, cattle were grazing on the richly verdant range. There was not a fence in sight in any direction.

"That place doesn't just look like a castle, Ki. It is one," Jessie said. "I have a feeling we've found the ranch of the late Lord Harrington."

"He certainly didn't spare any effort to make himself feel at home," Ki commented as they reached the path that led from the road to the castle.

"I imagine he needed a place like this to feel at home. Or maybe he just wanted to show his crude American cousins what an English nobleman was accustomed to at home," Jessie said. "I'm surprised that he left off the final touch, though."

"I don't see what it could be," Ki told her, studying the high, narrow, arched windows in their ornately carved stone embrasures and the broad entrance recessed in another arch of carved stone.

"There's no moat," Jessie told him. "After seeing the way the rest of the place looks, I'm surprised he left it off. And I'm very curious to see what it looks like inside."

"We'll soon find out," Ki said as they dismounted and went to the door. A massive iron ring hanging in front of a steel plate adorned one of the doors.

Ki was just reaching for it when the door swung open and a portly butler appeared in the opening. Before either Jessie or Ki could speak, the man said, "Lady Pamela has asked me to offer you her regrets that she is not receiving today. If you will be kind enough to—"

"Lady Pamela will change her mind when you give her my message," Jessie said. "I want you to listen carefully and repeat to her exactly what I'm about to tell you."

Recognizing the authority in Jessie's voice, the butler fell silent and nodded.

Jessie said, "I realize that we were not invited to call on Lady Pamela, but this isn't a social visit. My name is Jessica Starbuck. I didn't know until I got to Fort Collins that Lord Harrington had died. My business was really with him. But it's very important that I talk to Lady Pamela about an urgent business matter in which her late husband was engaged at the time of his death."

"With all respect, Miss Starbuck, this is hardly the time to—" the butler began to say.

Again Jessie interrupted him. "You are not the one to judge. Let your mistress make her own decision. Now, we'll wait here for you to deliver my message."

For a moment the butler stood silent, obviously debating

the wisdom of arguing with Jessie. Habit ruled, and he bowed to the voice of authority. With a stiff nod, he said, "Very well, Miss Starbuck. Please step inside. I will inform her ladyship of your arrival."

Moving back, the butler opened the door wider. Jessie and Ki went into the entry and, after an apologetic slight bow, the butler left.

Through the open door to the room beyond, Jessie could see the vaulted ceiling of the adjoining room, which would have been a bit small for a polo game but was certainly big enough for a tennis match to be played on its tile floor. As gloomy as the room was, its draperies drawn against the sun, Jessie could see that its furniture matched the chamber's enormous size. There were four divans and a dozen chairs, all of them with high backs and heavily upholstered, two or three small tables, and one table that could have seated a dinner party of twenty with room to spare.

Under her breath, Jessie said, "The late Lord Harrington obviously thought on a large scale, Ki. Unless he was tremendously rich in his own right, he'd need a great deal of money to build a palace like this and pay for its upkeep."

"From what we've learned of the cartel, we know it's very generous with its top operatives," Ki said. "And I gathered from the bits and pieces of talk I heard while I was in the hole that Harrington had paid them a chunk of cash for attacking that train we were on."

"We were lucky that he didn't get everything he paid for," Jessie said. "If we'd both been—" She broke off quickly as the butler's footsteps echoed.

When the butler entered, his face was expressionless. He bowed to Jessie and said, "Her ladyship has consented to see you, Miss Starbuck. And your, ah, your companion as well, of course. If you will be kind enough to come with me—" With a sweeping gesture of invitation, he turned and started through the room.

Exchanging glances, Jessie and Ki followed him, their heels echoing on the tiled floor. They went into a wide corridor broken by a half dozen closed doors and along it to an open door at its end. Stepping aside to allow them to enter first, the butler moved into the doorway and said, "Your guests, Lady Pamela. Miss Jessica Starbuck and her companion."

In contrast to the great chamber off the entry, this one was small, but roomy. It was sparsely furnished with only an oval table, a half dozen chairs, and a chaise longue. Its drapes were pulled aside to allow the last rays of the setting sun to stream in at an oblique angle. They struck a silken tapestry that covered one wall, and Ki's eyes opened when he saw that it was a priceless one. Its silk figures included five phoenixes intermingled with magnolias, peonies, bats as symbols of happiness, and fungi for good luck.

Jessie's attention had not been drawn to the screen. She'd centered it on the woman who sat on the chase longue, one arm propped against its back and the other lying across her thighs. Lady Pamela was a fair blonde, her hair very fine and pale. Her cheekbones were high, her nose aquiline, her lips full, and her chin firm. Her eyes were a very light blue, her cheeks a natural pink and free of cosmetics. She wore a pale blue silk kimono heavy with embroidery and did not rise when Jessie and Ki entered, but rather extended her hand to Jessie.

"I'm sorry to intrude on your privacy, Lady Pamela," Jessie said, "but the business I came to discuss with your late husband is very important to me. I didn't hear of Lord Harrington's death until we stopped at Fort Collins and—"

"Please, Miss Starbuck," Lady Pamela broke in with a small gesture of one hand, "there's no need for you to apologize. You must've traveled for some distance, and I assure you that I've gotten over the shock of his death.

Now, sit down and we will talk about your problem. If you would prefer to talk privately without your attendant present, Jenkins will be glad to take him to the servant's quarters."

"Ki is more than my attendant," Jessie said firmly. "He was my father's friend and companion for many years and is my friend and adviser as well. If you don't object, I'd prefer to have him stay."

"Of course," Lady Pamela said. She lifted a finger of the hand propped against the chaise and said, "Jenkins."

Hurriedly the butler placed chairs for Jessie and Ki and then vanished silently. Showing no embarrassment for her scrutiny, Lady Pamela studied her callers intently for several moments.

"I'm afraid you're going to be disappointed, Miss Starbuck, for I know nothing about my husband's business," she said at last. "He never discussed it with me and I never asked him to. He had just returned from an extended business trip two days before he died, and he'd spent most of his time in his study. I saw him only at mealtime."

"Surely you've looked at his papers—" Jessie began to say.

"No, Miss Starbuck," Pamela broke in. "In the early days of our marriage, he made it quite clear to me that I was not to question him or interfere in any way with the management of his finances. And I never did."

"It seems to me that you're going to be forced to learn how to manage the property he must have left you," Jessie stated.

"Not at all," Pamela replied. "His attorney and his banker are on the way here from Denver. I had a telegram from them this morning. They've been delayed, waiting for Sidney's younger brother Thomas, who inherits Sidney's title."

"Then your present situation is only temporary," Jessie

said. "In that case, we can talk later."

"Of course," Lady Pamela replied. "Luckily Thomas had gotten here from England just short of a month ago. When they get here and everything's settled, I shall employ them to manage my properties just as Sidney did. So, you see, Miss Starbuck, I shan't be forced to do anything that I haven't done in the past."

"You're very fortunate," Jessie told her. She stood up. "Ki and I will go back to town and put up at the hotel, Lady Pamela. We'll come back in a day or two and settle the business I came to see your husband about. If you're going to have your properties administered by the men who're coming, they're the ones I need to talk to."

"Of course," Pamela said. "But there's no need for you to leave. There are a dozen bedrooms here in the house— more than enough to accommodate you and the men who're arriving. You shall stay here—and your assistant as well, of course."

"Oh, no!" Jessie protested. "You'll be busy and—"

"Nonsense!" Lady Pamela interrupted. "I insist. It will make things much more convenient, and I shall be glad to have another woman here as my guest. Tell me you'll agree to stay. Please do! It—it hasn't been pleasant—alone except for the staff in this huge house."

"Since you put it that way, I'll be glad to," Jessie said. "I know what it means being alone in a situation such as you're facing."

"It's settled," Pamela said. "Now, I'll ring for Jenkins. We'll find a room for you and suitable accommodations for—what did you say his name is? Ki?"

"Yes. He's to me what your brother-in-law and your attorney and banker are to you, Lady Pamela."

"Of course. Now, we'll get you settled in. Then you and I must sit down and have a long chat."

★

Chapter 13

When the knock sounded at the door of the bedroom to which the butler had escorted her, Jessie was standing beside the bed, bending over the saddlebags. Sure that it was Ki who knocked, she did not go to the door, but called, "Come in." When she heard the knob click, she turned to the door and was surprised to see a middle-aged woman—chubby-faced, red-cheeked, and wearing the traditional white cap and black dress of a maid.

"Begging your pardon, miss," the woman said, "Her ladyship thought you might like a fresh dress to wear down to dinner, so she's sent you one of her own."

"That's very thoughtful," Jessie said. "Traveling by horseback doesn't allow me to carry much of a wardrobe."

The maid nodded. "Now, let's just slip this on, and I'll pin up a tuck here and there, and you'll be proper togged out before Jenkins rings the dinner chimes."

Pinning up a tuck here and there was a short job for the maid. When she'd finally finished, Jessie stepped to the mirror and smiled approvingly.

"That's very nice," she said. "Thank you for your help. Now, if you don't mind doing me another favor, I'd like for you to take a message to the gentleman who's with me."

"That'd be Ki," the maid said. "I'll go past his room on the way to my quarters. What shall I tell him, miss?"

"Just that I'd like to talk with him a minute or two before we go downstairs to dinner. You can tell him which room I'm in."

"No trouble at all, miss," the maid said.

Within five minutes, there was a light tapping on Jessie's door and she opened it to admit Ki. He stopped short when he saw Jessie in the dinner dress and said, "This is a real surprise! At first I couldn't believe it was you, Jessie. I thought I'd gone to the wrong room."

Unperturbed, Jessie replied, "Lady Pamela offered it to me, Ki. I couldn't very well refuse to wear it."

"You're going to make me look shabby," Ki said, indicating his loose black jacket and trousers.

"At least they're clean and neat, Ki," she said.

"They'll have to accept me the way I am."

Jessie smiled. The smile faded and she said, "I asked that maid to give you my message because I think we need to talk privately before we go to dinner. We're in the camp of the enemy here, Ki."

"You think the men who're coming with the new Lord Harrington will be cartel operatives, Jessie?"

"It's very likely. Of course, there's no way to be positive until we see how they react to our being here."

"Anybody high up in the cartel knows the Starbuck name," Ki pointed out. "They'll certainly recognize you."

"Oh, if they're cartel hirelings, I expect them to," she replied calmly.

"What do you think they'll do?"

"I've been trying to figure that out. Under the circumstances, I don't think they'll do anything rash. That's not the way the cartel operates."

"Are you sure that's the case now, Jessie?" Ki asked. "I've been wondering if we haven't put our heads in the lion's mouth by staying here."

"Our heads have been there before," Jessie reminded him. "We're not putting them in blindly this time, though. We know that Lord Harrington was in the cartel, so it's a pretty safe bet that his younger brother is. And even before seeing the men who're with him, I'm positive they must be, too."

"Yes, that's occurred to me," Ki said. "But so far I haven't been able to come up with any sort of plan. Have you?"

"No. I was hoping you might have. But perhaps this isn't the kind of situation we can plan for, Ki."

"It's certainly one we've never faced before," Ki stated. "About the only thing we're sure so far is that Harrington's widow doesn't have any connection with the cartel, but aside from you and me she might be the only person in this house who doesn't."

"We've got to find out more about the brother," Jessie said. "And get a look at that lawyer and the banker who're with him. All I can think of to do is to wait and see what happens at dinner, and—" Jessie stopped as a muted chiming sounded through the closed door. "That's the call to dinner," she said. "I suppose we'll just have to watch, wait, and hope we'll have time to work out some plan."

They went downstairs and along the hall. One of the doors that had been closed when Jessie and Ki walked along the corridor earlier stood open now, and the butler was in position outside it, waiting for the dinner guests. He bowed Jessie and Ki through the door. A long table spread with snowy linen occupied its center, and two waiters as erect as military sentries flanked the heavily laden sideboard at one end.

Lady Pamela stood across the long, narrow room in front of ceiling-high windows now hidden behind velvet curtains. Three men were grouped around her. She wore a shimmering satin dinner dress, and the men were clad in dinner jackets. When Pamela saw Jessie and Ki enter, she beckoned for them to join the group.

"Miss Starbuck," she said. "And Ki. Let me present my brother-in-law, Lord Thomas Harrington. And Sir Rufus Clendenning, who was my late husband's legal advisor, and Sir Albert Gray, our family banker."

While the formalities of introduction were being observed, Jessie took stock of the newcomers. The new Lord Harrington was a tall young man with blond hair that bunched into a cowlick in spite of the pomade that shone from it. His jaw was firm, his cheekbones high, his eyes a bright blue in a lightly tanned face.

Clendenning was both short and thin, and the thinness of his frame was reflected in his features. His chin came to a bony point and his nose was narrow from the eyebrows down to its tip. His lips were a pursed pink line, his dark hair a few stringy threads plastered to his scalp.

Gray was tall and thick. His face was tanned and had no really notable features except his mouth, which was large and had a pendulous lower lip. It drew attention from the rest of his face, which was so commonplace that it gave him the kind of anonymity that would make him the unnoticed man in a group of more than three.

He and the lawyer seemed to have agreed to sink into the background. Their handshakes were perfunctory. Immediately after Jessie had been introduced to him, Clendenning turned side and began a quiet conversation with his young client.

Jessie noticed that Ki was still talking to Lady Pamela. She tried to catch his eye, but failed, and to prolong the introduction process she turned back to Gray.

"Are you with one of the Denver banks?" she asked.

"To be quite precise, it's not really a Denver bank, Miss Starbuck. I manage the Denver office of the Imperial Bank of Canada," Gray replied. "There are a great many British citizens in the western states now, as I'm sure you know, and most of them tend to favor an English bank."

"Of course," Jessie said. Although she kept her face expressionless, she remembered instantly the trouble she'd had some time ago when the cartel had infiltrated the Montreal office of the Imperial Bank of Canada. Suspicious at once, but seeing no reason for allowing her surroundings and company to inhibit her, she went on, "I suppose you're familiar with the late Lord Harrington's business interests?"

"Oh, quite. He looked to us for advice as well as for financing when he needed it."

Jessie decided to take the plunge. Watching the banker closely without appearing to do so, she asked, "Did the late Lord Harrington ask your bank to finance him in buying a substantial amount of land in Wyoming?"

"Wyoming?" Gray asked. Then he shook his head. "It must be something that he didn't get around to discussing with me before his death. I've been out of my office for almost a month, Miss Starbuck. I didn't learn he'd passed away until I returned a few days ago."

"I see," Jessie replied, not knowing whether to feel frustrated or relieved.

"May I ask what your interest is?"

"I haven't any personal interest. But a friend, a man who was the foreman of my ranch for a long time, is trying to buy the same land Lord Harrington wanted." Jessie paused. "I stopped here to see if I could persuade him to—"

Before she could go on, Lady Pamela raised her voice.

"Let's sit down," Pamela said.

Her tone made her words an order rather than a light suggestion, and the group moved toward the table. Cards marked the seating arrangement. As fitted his new station, Lord Thomas sat at the head of the table with Jessie on his right and Gray on his left. Lady Pamela sat at the opposite end with Ki on her right and Clendenning on her left.

At the sideboard, Jenkins started the two waiters toward the table with soup tureens. As she joined the others in sipping the soup, Jessie unobtrusively studied the new Lord Harrington, wondering how he would be as an opponent in the battle with the cartel that she was sure lay just ahead.

Thomas seemed abstracted, thinking deeply, for half the time when Jessie turned to talk with him, his answers bore little or no relationship to the questions she asked. As course followed course, Jessie noticed that he paid as little attention to his food as he did to her and exchanged only an occasional word with Gray.

She finally decided that the young Briton's silence and strained manner was the result of his first realization of the responsibility that his inheritance would bring him. She devoted herself to watching the others while the meal went on, and she glanced occasionally at the sideboard where the butler was dispatching the waiters to the table with the successive courses. He took on the job of keeping the wineglasses filled.

Clendenning was as silent as Lord Thomas. Whenever Jessie turned to him and tried to begin a conversation, he answered her with a quick response and returned at once to his food. Jessie saw that Lady Pamela was chatting animatedly with Ki, turning only occasionally to exchange a few words with Clendenning.

At last the table was cleared of the dessert dishes and champagne glasses, and the butler wheeled to the table a

146

service cart that carried bottles of port, brandy, and the appropriate glasses as well as a cigar humidor. He glanced questioningly at Lady Pamela. When she nodded, the butler bowed to the diners and left the room, closing the door behind him.

As the latch clicked, Lady Pamela rose and surveyed her guests. "I do not intend to leave you men to drink your wine and brandy and smoke your cigars alone," she said. Turning to Jessie, she added, "Nor will I suggest that Miss Starbuck leave unless she chooses to do so."

Jessie shook her head, and Lady Pamela went on. "Perhaps this is not an appropriate time for me to say what I am planning to," she said. "But I think it will be better for me to speak now rather than to wait for my late husband's will to be read."

Jessie was looking around the table now while Pamela spoke. A puzzled frown puckered Gray's face, Clendenning was staring at Pamela with something approaching consternation, Ki sat impassive, and Lord Thomas was staring with his mouth open in astonishment.

"I have had time to think since Sidney died," Pamela said, "and after considering all the choices I have, I've decided that I will continue to live here at the ranch and operate it as I think he would have."

Pamela paused for breath, glanced around the table, and smiled at the listeners. Jessie had now decided that this must be a carefully rehearsed speech.

"But I know that a lone woman cannot do things that a man can," Pamela said, "so I intend to ask Thomas, now Lord Harrington, to stay and be my manager." Looking now directly at Thomas, she said, "It will be a lifetime job, Thomas. You will have full authority. Some day I hope that you will marry and raise a family who will—" She stopped and frowned as Clendenning rose to his feet. "Rufus, why are you interrupting me?" she asked.

"Because I can't let you go on," the lawyer answered. "The will Sidney left was supposed to be read tomorrow, but in view of what you've been saying, I'll have to tell you now."

"Tell me what?" Pamela asked when Clendenning paused.

"I'm afraid you don't have the authority to appoint Thomas as manager of this ranch," Clendenning said, "although he's to be in charge of the property. You see, Pamela, Sidney left you only dower rights in his will as he was required to by English law since you're both British citizens. Thomas inherits the ranch and the remainder of the estate."

"Dower rights!" Pamela exclaimed, disbelief in her voice. "But that means—"

Clendenning broke in hastily, his voice soothing. "You'll really have nothing to worry about, Pamela," he said. "Dower rights from an estate as large as Sidney left will assure you of getting several thousand pounds a year."

Lady Pamela's face had paled, but now an angry red flush crept up her throat and spread to her face. Her voice strained, she said, "I shan't stand for this!" She turned to stare at Gray. "Albert, you were Sidney's financial adviser. You must have known about his plan!"

"I'm afraid I did, Pamela," Gray stated.

"And you allowed him to cheat me?" she asked.

"He hasn't cheated you!" Gray replied. "In fact, he—"

Thomas leaped to his feet and broke in, "Stop this arguing!" He turned to Lady Pamela. "I knew nothing about the plans until I got to Denver, Pam, and ever since Mr. Clendenning told me of the will, I've been thinking things over, trying to decide what to do."

"It seems to me that Sidney's decided for both of us," she said, her voice trembling and unsteady.

"Not if we don't like it!" Thomas replied. "Damn it,

148

I'm an Englishman! I don't want to live in America, and I don't want to own this ranch! As far as I'm concerned, you can have it."

"That's impossible!" Clendenning exclaimed. "The will can't be changed, young man! Not by you or Pamela or anyone else!"

"Then when the ranch is transferred to me, I'll deed it to Pamela, or do whatever else it takes to get it off my hands!" Thomas retorted hotly.

"Now, be practical!" Gray urged. "Thomas, if you persist in trying to undo what Sidney wished, his estate will be tied up in legal proceedings for years!"

"I don't see why," the young man retorted. "If he left the ranch to me, I own it. If I want to give away what's mine, I certainly have that right!"

"I'm afraid it's not that simple," Clendenning told him. "You see, Thomas, there are other factors involved."

"What other factors?" Pamela broke in. "If Thomas doesn't want the ranch and I do, why can't he give it to me?"

Clendenning shook his head. "Because I'm quite certain the mortgage holders would not approve such a transfer."

"Mortgage holders!" Pamela said. "What are you talking about, Rufus? I thought Sidney owned the ranch!"

"Perhaps you did," Clendenning answered. "But the fact is that there is a mortgage, Pamela, and it requires the annual payment of a very substantial sum. Albert can tell you that."

"I'm afraid Rufus is right, Pamela," Gray said. "There have been several times through the years when the cattle market was depressed and Sidney had to secure loans from the bank in order to meet the mortgage payments."

"But surely there were good years when he paid those old mortgages off!" Pamela protested.

"Not enough good years to offset the bad ones, I'm

afraid," Gray said. "There's still a very substantial sum outstanding. As long as Sidney was in charge, we advanced the money because we had full confidence in him. I'm not at all sure that our board would continue to approve loans of the size required if you were in charge."

Jessie had been following the conversation with a great deal of interest. She had concealed her close attention, even though those engaged in the discussion were paying no attention to her. Now and then she and Ki had exchanged glances, their years of close companionship making words unnecessary.

She was sure by now that Ki understood the situation as well as she did. The Imperial Bank of Canada had at last fallen completely into the hands of the cartel. In spite of the late Lord Harrington's willing cooperation, the scheming cartel masters had not trusted him completely and had secured the cartel's hold with the mortgages that had come to the surface so suddenly and unexpectedly.

Now, having lost their front, the cartel intended to hold securely to this portion of the web it was trying to spin, a web that would give it a firm hold on the economic strength of America. Jessie decided that the time had come for her to take a hand, to use her huge resources if necessary to prevent a cartel takeover of such a key portion of the American West.

Using Gray's remark as her opening, she said to him, "If I might make a suggestion, Sir Albert, in case your bank isn't willing to carry the mortgages under the new Lord Harrington's management of the ranch, I would be willing to buy them from your bank. I have some knowledge of ranching, and I'm sure that I could turn this ranch into a steadily profitable operation."

150

★

Chapter 14

Jessie's words were as effective as a magic wand in turning the group into statues. The room was instantly silent as everyone except Ki stared at her. Gray found his voice first, and when he spoke, his voice matched the frown that was growing on his face.

"If you have an idea that my bank will surrender the mortgages of an old and valued client, Miss Starbuck, I'm afraid you've miscalculated," he said. "I can assure you that the directors would do no such thing!"

"But you've just hinted that your bank would foreclose the mortgages instead of renewing them," Jessie reminded him.

"Nonsense!" Gray snorted. "You're putting a false interpretation on my words!"

"Then Lord Thomas and Lady Pamela haven't anything to worry about, have they?" she asked sweetly. "They have the option—"

"Miss Starbuck!" Clendenning broke in. "And Sir Albert! I find this discussion most upsetting! I suggest that both of you reserve any further exchanges until I have had time to review this unhappy matter with Lady Pamela and Lord Thomas. And I have no intention of speaking with them until they have had time to recover from the shock of this unfortunate misunderstanding and to consider their positions very carefully!"

"I suppose that means tomorrow?" Gray asked.

"At the very earliest," Clendenning replied. "Perhaps not even then, but certainly by the following day."

"That suits me," Thomas said quickly. "If Pamela agrees—"

"Of course, I do," Pamela said. "But you can be sure that I don't intend to stand by quietly while—"

"Lady Pamela!" Clendenning interrupted. "Please don't prolong this further. You'll see things differently after you've recovered from the shock you just had."

"Perhaps I will," Pamela said. Looking quickly around the table, she added, "All of you know how to find your way back to your rooms. I'll bid you good night now."

For a moment after Pamela had left the room, those remaining gazed at one another silently. Then Jessie turned to go and Ki followed her. As they walked toward the door, Jessie said in a low voice, "We'd better talk, Ki. Let's go outside. We can walk a little way from the house where there's no chance we'll be overheard. I need a breath of fresh air anyhow."

Ki nodded. They turned to the left as they left the room and walked down the corridor to the entry. The massive front door was unlocked, and they stepped outside into a night of brilliant starlight under an unclouded sky.

"What did you think of the surprise?" Jessie asked as they strolled down the veranda steps.

"Two things impressed me, Jessie," Ki replied. "The first was that the late lord's trusted financial adviser doesn't seem to be at all interested in protecting Lady Pamela."

"Yes," Jessie said. "Of course, some loyalties can't be transferred easily."

"True," Ki stated. "But I'd think it would be fairly easy for Gray to support the position of the young, attractive widow of a man who's been a long-term associate."

"You have a point, Ki," she said. "What was the other thing that caught your attention?"

"That Gray hasn't transferred any loyalty to the new Lord Thomas, either."

"I noticed that, too. But I'm sure you remember our own past experience with the Imperial Bank of Canada."

"Perhaps not as vividly as you do since it was you their men kidnapped. Even then, the bank was secretly controlled by the cartel."

"My guess is that the bank has quite likely become a full cartel partner by now, even if it wasn't when we had our own troubles with it," Jessie suggested.

"Yes. The cartel has a way of absorbing businesses that will help it gain its objectives."

"We'll have to stop Gray from getting control of the Harrington holdings. From everything we've found out so far, he managed to get his hands on much more land than we realized," Jessie said soberly. "With the bank's money and resources, he was certainly trying to push into Wyoming."

"Just how will we start, Jessie?"

"I don't know yet. But I'll be thinking about it between now and tomorrow morning. You will, too, I'm sure."

"Naturally."

"We'll compare notes before breakfast. Now, we'd better go back inside, or we might find the front door's been locked for the night. I wouldn't want to arouse any suspicion at this point."

They turned back to the house and found the door had

not been locked. At the end of the corridor, they parted and started for their own rooms. Ki opened his door and to his surprise found the room in darkness, though he'd left the lamp on the bureau burning. He opened the door wider to let the light from the hall shine into it while he relighted the lamp.

"Don't light the lamp, Ki," a woman's voice said in a half whisper. "And close the door, please. I need to talk with you privately."

From the first words he heard, Ki had recognized the voice as Pamela's. He said nothing. He closed the door and stood quietly to let his eyes adjust to the room's darkness, and as they did, he saw her sitting on the edge of his bed. She'd changed from the elaborate outfit she'd worn at dinner into a clinging, filmy negligee.

"I desperately need someone to talk to," Pamela said, "and you know I can't turn to Rufus or Albert. So much happened at dinner that I'm all upset and confused."

"Wouldn't it be better if you talked with Jessie?" Ki suggested. "She'd understand your problems better than I might."

"No," Pamela replied. "I thought about going to her. I know she's very smart, but she'd only be able to give me the viewpoint of another woman. I need advice from a man who'd understand the way Thomas might be thinking. Please come sit down by me where we can talk very quietly. In this house, I never know when one of the servants might be listening at the keyhole."

In spite of his misgivings, Ki sat down on the edge of the bed. He said, "I'm flattered that you should think of me, Lady Pamela. But Sir Rufus Clendenning was your husband's lawyer. I'm not a lawyer or banker or anything of the kind."

"Oh, Rufus wouldn't be able to see anything but legalities! And you heard what Albert said. His bank comes first, regardless of the fact that Sidney and I were his friends."

"Perhaps it wouldn't be possible for me to see things from your viewpoint, either, Lady Pamela," Ki said soberly. "Or do you know that Jessie and I didn't exactly consider your husband one of our friends?"

"I don't think he was my friend or even much of a husband, especially after what happened tonight in the dining room," Pamela replied. "But friends don't see each other clearly. What I need now is to understand what he was thinking when he made that stupid will. And how Rufus could advise him to shut me out. And why Albert Gray has kept silent all these years about Sidney's plan. I'm all at sea about everything right now."

"I'm still not sure—" Ki began to say.

Pamela cut in quickly. "When Jessie and I were talking earlier, she mentioned that you'd been with her father for a long time, and I'm sure you learned a great deal from him. She also told me that she looks on you as her friend and adviser as well. Even if I'm not sure your relationship stops there, that doesn't—"

"Lady Pamela," Ki interrupted, "Jessie told you the exact truth. I am proud that she calls me her friend, and I do not expect or wish for her to be more than that. Jessie understands this as clearly as I do."

"You sound very convincing," Pamela said. "I really think I can believe you, Ki. Will you help me? I won't ask you to do a thing that would harm Jessie in any way. I promise you that."

"Even without your promise, I couldn't do anything that would possibly affect Jessie," Ki told her. Since he'd learned the object of Pamela's visit, Ki had been analyzing the problem that faced him. He could see no harm in listening to her and thought he might get some information that could be of help in defeating the cartel's objectives. He

155

said, "Go ahead. Ask me whatever you like. I'll try to answer."

"Perhaps if you could help me understand why Sidney treated me the way he did—" Pamela began to say and then let her voice trail off to silence.

"Probably your husband had been ill for quite some time and wasn't aware how serious his condition was," Ki suggested.

"He didn't act like a sick man—as far as caring for the ranch was concerned. His one interest was adding more land to what he had. Lately, he'd been going off on trips to Denver and Wyoming."

"Did he always go alone?"

"If you mean did he take me with him, the answer is no. He did make several trips with Albert, but I just assumed he'd need him on hand to give him financial advice."

"His trips were to buy land?" Ki asked.

"Most of them seemed to be. He didn't always confide in me, Ki. He'd get a letter or telegram and be gone."

"And you didn't know who sent the letters and telegrams?"

"Not always. But almost always when he came back, he'd say something about Albert. I suppose he needed money from the bank for whatever reason he'd made the trip."

Ki was beginning to see a pattern unfold, and it indicated Lord Harrington's subservience to the cartel. He asked, "Who looked after the ranch while he was away?"

"Why, the foreman, of course. Joe Bryan. Oh, Bryan would come to the house and ask me a question now and then, but when Sidney was away, he did pretty much as he pleased."

After a moment of silent thought, Ki said, "Pamela, I'm sure your husband treated you just as so many Englishmen treat women—as though they're children who can't be relied on to handle business matters."

"But I'm not an Englishwoman!" Pamela protested. "My mother was French! Even though my father was English, she handled the money in our house."

"Did you ever tell your husband you wanted to share in the way he operated the ranch or his other business affairs?"

"I tried to. He patted me on the head—" She stopped and then said, "No, I'll be truthful. It was my bottom he patted. But he didn't pay any attention to me—outside of bed." She hesitated a moment and then added, "And very little attention there for more than a year—since he got this craze to add more land to what he already owned."

"Sick men do strange things sometimes—such as neglecting a wife no matter how attractive she might be."

"Then you think I'm attractive, Ki?"

"Of course, I do." As he spoke, Ki realized where Pamela had begun to lead their conversation and searched his mind for a way to steer it in another direction.

As fast as Ki's brain worked, Pamela's fingers worked faster. While he was still speaking, her hand darted to his crotch and fumbled for his fly. When she found nothing but a seam in the front of his trousers, she slid her fingers lower on his crotch, and by the time Ki closed his own hand around her wrist, she'd already succeeded in her quest. Her hand cradled Ki's quiescent shaft for a moment. Then she grasped it firmly.

"Don't say no to me, Ki, or push me away," she pleaded, her eyes shining through the gloom as he looked up at him. "I've needed a man for such a long time!"

He wanted to respond to the continued pulsing pressures of Pamela's hands, but did not allow himself to become erect. Though he was sure after her outburst at dinner that

157

she knew nothing of her dead husband's cartel connection, he had no intention of falling into a trap baited by sex. Then it occurred to him to fight fire with fire. He allowed himself to begin a slow erection.

Pamela gasped when she felt Ki's shaft begin to swell. She renewed her efforts to free it from his clothing, and this time Ki helped her. He lifted himself from the bed long enough to slip the waistband of his loose trousers down his hips. When Pamela realized what he was doing, she released him and added her hands to his. Her fingers found the folded scarf which Ki wore beneath his trousers, and she tugged at the narrow cloth until it slid down his thighs with his trousers.

"That's better," Pamela whispered as her hands returned to seek the bared cylinder their efforts had released. She closed her soft hand around the firming flesh, held Ki cradled for a moment, and then squeezed him gently. "But you're not ready yet. I'll help you."

Bending above Ki, Pamela found his lips with hers and they clung in a long lover's kiss. Her tongue opened Ki's lips and darted between them to entwine with his. Ki relaxed and lay back across the bed. He slipped his hands between the folds of her negligee, sought her breasts, and found them. Then he began to caress them with his fingers while Pamela shuddered in response to his gentle rasping of her blossomed rosettes.

Her hands were still exploring Ki's crotch. With a sudden move, she slid from Ki's arms and knelt beside the bed. Ki had allowed himself to grow firmer. Pamela bowed her head and Ki felt the moist warmth of her tongue as she began to caress him gently. As Ki let himself continue to swell and harden in response to her attentions, he felt her wet, warm lips close over him—then the gentle, persistent rasping of her tongue as her mouth engulfed him.

Stretching his arms to reach her, Ki slid Pamela's loose

negligee off her shoulders. When it slid to the floor, he moved his hands to her large, firm breasts and began caressing the globes and their protruding tips. Pamela's body was writhing now, and Ki realized that the time had come to carry their caresses to a climax. He slid his hands into her armpits, lifted her bodily to the bed, and held her suspended above him.

Pamela grasped Ki's intention at once. She threw one leg across his hips to straddle him and reached down to position the tip of his rigid shaft. Ki lowered her slowly as Pamela twisted her hips from side to side while she sank down until Ki was buried fully. Pamela was motionless for a moment. Then with a throaty cry she began rotating her hips in wild gyrations that Ki matched with lusty thrusts.

Her frenzy was too urgent to last more than a few minutes. Pamela's body started quivering, her hips began jerking, and strangled, small screams burst from her throat as she went into her climax. Ki grasped her hips and held her locked to his as he thrust upward with slow, steady strokes. After a final scream and a wild burst of ecstatic jerks of her hips, Pamela suddenly went limp and sagged to rest her quivering form on Ki's muscular body.

Ki had not allowed himself to join Pamela in climaxing. He held her clasped in his arms until her shudders rippled, faded, and died away. She was inert. For several minutes Pamela lay quietly on his chest, breathing in broken gasps. Then her body stopped heaving and she stirred and turned her lips until they were close to Ki's ear.

"You know now how badly I needed to have a man inside me," she whispered. "But I never thought it'd be a man like you, Ki. I can still feel you, big and hard."

"We've just begun," Ki assured her. "After you've rested, we'll—"

"I don't need to rest," Pamela interrupted. "Feeling you in me just makes me want to start again."

"Then we won't wait," Ki told her.

Lifting Pamela's lax body with him, Ki moved them until the bed supported the full length of their prone bodies. Without breaking their joining, he held Pamela to him as he rolled to get above her. Pamela voiced a deep, throaty sigh of anticipation when she felt Ki's body weighing down on her. She spread her thighs wide as he lifted his hips to begin thrusting again. As he surged down with a fierce lunge, she locked her ankles above his back and pulled herself up to meet his lusty stroke.

"Fast, Ki!" she said, gasping with each urgent word. "And don't stop, even if I beg you to!"

Ki responded to Pamela's breathless request. He drove again and again. She rocked beneath him, moaning with each downward lunge. Far sooner than he'd expected, Pamela's body began trembling again, and after a few more of his deep thrusts, she started crying out. The frantic quivering of her body began once more.

Suddenly she cried out loudly, but the gyrations of her hips did not stop. They kept on, one following the other, until the last frenzied cry of fulfillment burst from her lips and she lay quivering and motionless. Ki kept on with his steady stroking until Pamela was once more joining him, her hips rising high to match the tempo of his downward drives.

At last she gasped, "Will you come with me this time, Ki?"

Ki did not stop his rhythmic lunges, but slowed his tempo to a more deliberate pace as he told her, "Of course, if you want me to."

"You mean you can still keep on?"

"For a while—if that's what you'd like."

"I'd not only like it, I'd love it, but I can't stand it much longer," Pamela gasped.

160

"Whenever you're ready, then," Ki said.

Pamela nodded, sighed, and closed her eyes. Ki speeded up again, and for a while she matched his faster tempo. Then she began trembling, and Ki knew her time was near. He pounded harder, thrusting as deeply as possible while Pamela's body began quivering.

Ki waited until her screams began, and as they reached a crescendo, he released his control. Pamela was in her final throes now, and when Ki began jetting, he slowed his thrusting to match her fading response. When Pamela finally lay still, Ki allowed himself to relax and lowered himself gently on her soft body until her shuddering came to an end. They both lay quietly.

Minutes ticked away, broken only by the sound of their breathing. Then Pamela said, "You happened along at just the right time, Ki. I knew I needed a man, but I didn't realize how badly. Now maybe I can think clearly about my problems."

"Your husband's will and Thomas's refusal to take the ranch?"

"Yes. And how deeply Sidney was in debt to that Canadian bank. And whether I can trust the two men I've always thought of as my friends. And—oh, a few other things as well."

"Talk to Jessie, Pamela," Ki advised. "She knows about cattle ranching and business, and I'm sure she'll be able to give you sound advice. You can talk to her as one woman talks to another."

"You don't think she'll suspect that you and I—"

Ki broke in before Pamela could complete her question. "I told you the truth, Pamela. I serve Jessie because of the many things her father did for me before his death. We have never been lovers and never will be."

"I'll talk to her the first thing in the morning," Pamela

161

promised. "And it must be getting very late. I'd better go to my suite, even if I'd rather stay here with you."

Pamela slipped off the bed, pulled her negligee around her, and slid silently through the door.

Chapter 15

Jessie drew the heavy drapes that hung over the windows of her bedroom and looked at the cattle grazing on the rolling land that stretched away to the eastern horizon. The sun was up, but still hanging low in the cloudless sky. As she watched, a cowhand came in sight, riding around the corner of the huge main house and heading for the grazing steers. When he got close to the scattered herd, he started reining his pony from side to side, riding in a small arc to start the cattle bunching ahead of him.

A steer broke from the herd he was forming, and the cowhand wheeled his mount toward the animal and dug his heels into the pony's flanks to speed it up. He quickly closed the gap between himself and the drifting steer and turned it back to the herd. Then he went on methodically with his job of hazing the scattered cattle.

Jessie watched the man during the short time required for him to shape up the steers and start them moving toward the horizon. Then she turned from the window with a sigh. The scene had reminded her of the Circle Star, and the thought of Sun waiting there in his corral for her return stirred a momentary desire to return to the ranch at once.

Then the disciplined mind she'd inherited from Alex took control. Jessie banished thoughts of the Circle Star and began thinking of the job that remained to be finished. She slipped quickly into her clothes and started for the door. She was reaching for the knob when a light tapping sounded on its panel. Opening the door, she greeted Ki with a smile.

"It's a beautiful day, Ki," she said. "Have you looked outside yet?"

Ki shook his head. "It didn't occur to me to. Why?"

"Oh, nothing special. I was just watching one of the hands work a bunch of steers and noticed how green the range is here compared to what we have on the Circle Star. I can understand why Lady Pamela would like to keep it."

"That's one of the things we need to talk about privately, Jessie," Ki said. "Has she come to ask you for help in working out her problems?"

"She has a lawyer to help her," Jessie said. "I'm a stranger. Why should she come to me?"

"Because I suggested it," Ki replied. "She was waiting in my room when I went in last night. I suppose she didn't feel that she could trust her brother-in-law or Gray or Clendenning after that scene at dinner."

"I see," Jessie said. "So far she hasn't followed your suggestion."

"I'm sure she will sometime during the day. Apparently her late husband didn't talk with her at all about business or what he was doing with the ranch. And I'm sure she still doesn't realize that he was connected with the cartel. Naturally, I didn't mention the cartel to her at all."

"Of course not," Jessie said, frowning thoughtfully. "If

164

she didn't come to me last night, then she probably will come today. I'll be thinking about what I should say to her. Now, we'd better go down and see if we can find some breakfast, Ki. In spite of that heavy dinner last night, I'm hungry."

"I could use some food. Let's go."

In the dining room, silver chafing dishes stood in line on the buffet. Pamela and Thomas were seated at the table, picking at the food on their plates. Both seemed relieved when Jessie and Ki came in.

"We're very informal at breakfast," Pamela told them after salutations had been exchanged. "Please help yourselves and come join us."

Passing up the porridge, eggs fried until they were brown and stiff, the thick slabs of ham and the pudgy sausages, Jessie and Ki helped themselves to scrambled eggs, bacon, and biscuits and then sat down.

"I hope you slept well," Thomas said stiffly as Jessie settled into the chair across from him.

"Yes, I did," she replied. "It was nice to be in a comfortable bed after all the traveling and camping out Ki and I have been doing for the past few weeks."

"I hope that being exposed to our family problems at dinner yesterday didn't upset you," Thomas stated. "If everything goes well, we should have our differences settled today. Pamela and I have been talking, and as soon as Sir Rufus and Sir Albert join us, we're going to confer with them to see if we can't come to some sort of agreement."

"Where are they?" Pamela inquired. "They've both been our guests here often enough in the past to know when breakfast is served."

"Don't fret, Pamela," Thomas said. "They'll be here in a few—" He broke off as a piercing scream broke the quiet of the room. "What the devil's that?"

165

"It came from upstairs," Pamela said. She stood up. "I'll just go and—" A second scream, louder than the first, interrupted her.

Pamela started toward the door, but before she could reach it, the maid who'd fitted Jessie with the borrowed dress rushed into the dining room.

"Lady Pamela!" the maid gasped. "It's Sir Rufus!"

"What about him, Gladys?" Pamela asked.

"Dead, ma'am! Layin' stark in bed with blood all over everywhere!"

Jessie and Ki leaped to their feet. Thomas had already risen. He started toward Pamela with Jessie and Ki following. They brushed past the maid as Pamela turned and moved to the door with Thomas close behind her.

"I wonder what's become of Gray?" Ki asked Jessie in a low voice as they started upstairs. "If he'd been in his room, the maid's screaming would certainly have brought him out."

"There's an outside possibility that he may be dead, too," Jessie answered in a half-whispered tone. "But from what we know about the Imperial Bank of Canada and what we heard at the dinner table last night, I've an idea that he's gone."

"After killing Clendenning?" Ki asked.

"That was my first thought. Of course, I might be wrong, but—" Jessie stopped as they reached the top of the stairs.

A few feet down the corridor, Pamela was standing in the hall and peering through an open door. Jessie and Ki stopped beside her.

"Don't look," Pamela said. "It's ghastly!"

Jessie and Ki brushed past Pamela and went into the room. In spite of their brushes with death in the course of their continuing struggle against the merciless killers of the

166

cartel, they found that Lady Pamela's description fit well what they saw.

Thomas was standing beside the bed and looking down at the small, huddled form of Sir Rufus Clendenning. The lawyer's glassy eyes bulged from their sockets, and his face was covered with streaks of blood and gray brain tissue. The top of his head was flattened where the bullet that killed him had literally blown off the top half of his skull.

"A lead bullet from a pistol pressed to the back of his head," Ki said to Jessie in a whisper.

"Yes," she said, "an executioner's shot." Turning to face the others, she asked. "I suppose no one heard a shot last night?"

"If the door to this room were closed, it's not likely any of us would've heard a thing. This room and Albert's, next to it, are the only ones occupied in this wing. Albert would've heard a shot, but it's not likely the rest of us would."

In the silence that followed, Jessie asked quietly, "But has anyone seen Sir Albert this morning?"

Pamela's jaw dropped and she gasped, "Oh, no! You don't suppose he's dead, too?"

"I'll go look in his room," Ki volunteered.

"I hope you—" She stopped when Ki hurried away. She turned to Jessie. "What could've happened, Jessie? Why did Rufus kill himself?"

"He didn't," Jessie told her. "He was shot in the back of the head. There's no way in the world that he could have held a gun in the position required to do the damage that was done. Besides, if he'd committed suicide, the gun would be here. I don't see one. Do you?"

"I–I didn't look," Pamela stammered. "And I don't want to look now, but—"

"There's no gun here," Thomas announced, turning

away from the bed with its grisly burden. "Sir Rufus was murdered."

Ki returned just in time to hear what Thomas told Jessie and Pamela. He added quickly, "And since Sir Albert Gray's not in his room and his luggage is gone, I don't think we have to do much guessing about who committed the murder."

"Not Albert!" Pamela protested. "He and Rufus have always been the best of friends!"

"Friendship sometimes takes second place to money," Ki said quietly. "Especially when there's a great deal of money and other important considerations at stake."

"I–I'm afraid I don't understand," Pamela said.

"You will later, I'm sure," Jessie said quickly. "Now, it seems to me that you and I can't be of much use here, Pamela. Let's go to your room where we'll be out of the way. Let Ki and Lord Thomas handle things here."

"But, I say—" Thomas began to say.

Ki cut him off. "Jessie's right, Lord Thomas. If things of this kind are strange to you, I've encountered similar situations before and I'll be glad to help."

"I–I really don't know where to begin," Thomas confessed after Jessie and Pamela had left. "Murder's not an everyday occurrence at home, you know."

"You'll find the American West quite different from England in that respect, Lord Thomas. There was no law here for so many years that honest people had to look out for themselves. We still do to some extent."

"What do we do first?"

"There's nothing we can do to help Sir Rufus, so I suggest we just pull the bedspread over him, and as soon as we're through here, we can send one of the hands for the undertaker."

As they drew the bedspread over the body, Thomas said, "If you don't mind, Ki, I'd prefer not to be addressed

168

with a title I have no intention of using. Just call me Thomas. Or, perhaps Tom would be better since everyone in the States seems to go by some sort of nickname."

"Of course," Ki said. "Now, Tom, suppose we look around and see if there's anything in Clendenning's baggage that might tell us why Gray did it. We might also get a hint where he'd run to hide."

"Isn't it likely he'd have gone to Denver?" Thomas asked. "It was his home."

"It's logical," Ki said, "but before we go there, we'd better look in Sir Rufus' baggage. There might be papers in it that would give us a clue as to any argument that had developed between him and Gray."

"Quite so," Thomas said. "But in England there's a law against trifling with evidence at the scene of a crime. Isn't there such a law here?"

"Oh, yes. But it won't do any harm to stretch the law a little if what we find gives us a lead," Ki said.

He looked around the room. There was no door that marked a closet and no sign of a valise, but a wardrobe standing against the wall opposite the bed seemed a likely place to begin searching.

Ki went to it, opened the drawers one by one, and found nothing in them except a shirt, underwear, socks, and a few handkerchiefs. He opened another compartment. A suit was on the rod that ran across the top; a pair of shoes, a valise, and a briefcase stood on the bottom. He picked up the suitcase, but its light weight told him at once that it was empty. When he picked up the briefcase, it yawned open of its own weight, and a quick glance showed him that it also was empty.

"But that's impossible!" Thomas said. He'd been standing behind Ki and looking over his shoulder. "When we left Denver that briefcase was bulging!"

"That leads us to a conclusion," Ki said. "If Sir Albert

did kill Sir Rufus, it was to get his hands on the papers that were in this briefcase."

"I say, Ki! That's brilliant!" Thomas exclaimed. "It's a bit like a story I read by one of your American writers, a chap named Poe. There was this detective in Paris—"

"Yes, I've read the story myself," Ki said. "But we can talk about it later. Right now we'd better go next door and see if we can find anything in Gray's room. I didn't take time to search it a while ago when I looked into it. The bed hadn't been slept in, so I assumed Gray had gone off sometime during the night."

They went into the next room, a mirror image of the one they'd just left. Ki went at once to the bureau and opened its drawers one by one. All of them were empty as was the wardrobe. As he closed the wardrobe door and turned back to Thomas, he noticed the fireplace. It was piled high with the fragile black ashes left by burned paper.

"I think that's the explanation we've been looking for," Ki said, pointing to the heaped hearth.

"Ashes?" Thomas frowned as he stared at the fireplace. Then his eyebrows went up and he went on. "Oh, I see! I really do see, Ki! Sir Albert burned the papers that were in Sir Rufus' briefcase!"

"After he'd read them, I imagine," Ki said. "Though as close as he and Pamela's husband seemed to be, I doubt there was anything in them that he wouldn't already have known."

"But isn't it likely there were documents in it about which Pamela and I might not have known?" Thomas asked. "Of course! There must've been! And that's why he shot Sir Rufus!"

"Your deduction's the same as mine," Ki said. "And I think we've found the reason he shot the lawyer. I'd guess that right now Gray's headed for Denver where he'll very likely try to destroy any duplicates of those burned documents."

"Is there any way that we can catch him?" Thomas asked.

"None I can—" Ki began to say and then stopped. "Let's go talk to Jessie, Tom. We might have an ace that we can play."

"Beg pardon?" Lord Thomas frowned.

"Come along," Ki said. "I'll explain while we're going down the hall to Pamela's room." As they walked down the corridor, Ki said, "You don't play poker, I suppose?"

His face showing his bewilderment, Thomas shook his head. "I know it's an American gambling game, but I'm not a gambler. In whist, I know the ace is an honors card, so I'm sure it must also be a high card in your country's poker."

"It is," Ki said. "And in one kind of poker the players get a hand of four cards face up, one card face down. That one is called a hole card."

"I see now," Thomas said.

Ki nodded as they reached the door of Lady Pamela's bedroom.

Ki knocked and Pamela called, "Yes? Come in."

Ki opened the door. Jessie and Pamela were seated beside the window. A small table between them held a teapot and cups. Jessie needed only to glance at Ki and Thomas to see that they'd discovered something of importance.

"What did you find, Ki?" she asked.

"Sir Albert's flown the coop," Ki said quickly. "He's burned many of Clendenning's papers. I imagine he's taken some with him. And the chances are he's headed for Denver. Do you know whether Longarm's in Denver or out on a case?"

"Now, Ki, you know I haven't any idea," Jessie said.

"Longarm moves around so much that I don't even try to keep in touch with him. But I understand why you're asking. Suppose we ride into Fort Collins right away and send him a telegram."

"That's what I was thinking," Ki said.

Pamela had been listening to the rapid exchange between Ki and Jessie. She said, "I haven't the slightest idea who this Longarm you're talking about might be, but from what you said, Jessie, I get the idea that he's a policeman of some kind. If—"

"He's a federal marshal," Jessie said, "and he doesn't let legal distinctions about jurisdiction stand in his way when he's after a criminal."

"And you know him well enough to ask him to arrest Albert?"

"Yes, of course," Jessie said. "But can we get a telegram to him in time?"

"I think you can," Pamela said. "He'd have had to go to Greeley to catch a train, and he couldn't have reached there early enough to get on the night express. The local didn't pass through Greeley until about an hour ago. It gets to Denver at noon. If you and Ki hurry, Jessie, I'm sure your friend will get the wire in time to be at the depot when the train gets in."

"Let's go, Ki," Jessie said. "It's only a short distance to Fort Collins. We should have plenty of time."

"There are times when I don't mind waiting," Jessie said to Ki as they walked across the street to the telegraph office for their third visit of the day. "But there are times like this when I resent every minute of waiting because I can only think of it as time wasted."

"Which it is, of course," Ki said. "But we don't want to leave before we know whether Longarm got your message."

"If he hasn't been sent away from Denver on a case, he's surely gotten it by now," Jessie said. "And he'd have been at the depot to arrest Gray. It's almost four o'clock."

They reached the ramshackle building that housed the local telegraph office and went inside. The clerk looked up from his desk behind the counter, and for the first time since their initial visit, he smiled.

"This time I got the answer to that message you sent, Miss Starbuck," he said. He reached to one side of the desk and took out a sheet of telegraph paper. "It cleared the wire not ten minutes ago."

"Thank you," Jessie said. Her eyes were on the message she was unfolding. She scanned it quickly and handed it to Ki. "I can't understand this, Ki."

Ki read the message: Sorry. Your man not on train. Need more help? C. Long.

Looking up, Ki said, "If Longarm didn't find Sir Arthur Gray on that train, he wasn't on it, Jessie."

"I agree with you, of course," she said. "Longarm's had too much experience to make a mistake in a simple job such as arresting a man whom I described as completely as I did in my wire."

"Do you think we might've jumped to the wrong conclusion when we decided that Gray would go back to Denver?"

"I suppose anything's possible, Ki," Jessie said. "But the most likely thing is that Gray had planned to kill Sir Arthur from the beginning and had his escape planned as well. We've seen the cartel men disappear this way before."

"There's not much point in going to Denver," Ki said thoughtfully. "We might as well start back to the ranch. If we don't waste any time, we can be there before dark."

Brushing their disappointment aside, they mounted their horses and started back. They said very little as their horses moved at an easy pace over the rolling rises and into the shadowed hollows, the setting sun at their backs. They topped a rise and got their first glimpse of the turrets of the main house.

Jessie turned in her saddle and leaned toward Ki to make a remark about the structure's being out of place in the Colorado countryside. The bullet that sang by her like an angry hornet missed her by an inch. Then from the rise ahead of them, the report of the rifle that had fired the slug reached their ears.

Chapter 16

Jessie and Ki had been the targets of surprise attacks too many times in the past to need any exchange of words. Before the echo of the rifle shot had died away, both were digging their heels into the flanks of their horses and bending low over the necks of their mounts to make themselves less visible targets. Jessie reined her pony to the right; Ki took his to the left.

They were two or three yards apart and moving in different directions when the next slug whistled between them. It was followed by the report of the sniper's rifle. The nearest cover Jessie saw was a small knoll fifty feet off the road. She made for it and reached it as another shot cut the air. This time the slug was so far off that Jessie could not hear its menacing whistle.

When Jessie reached the knoll, she was sliding out of her saddle even before the horse had responded to her tug on the reins. Dropping flat as she landed, she crawled behind the little rise and then looked around for Ki. She did not see him, but saw his horse standing a hundred yards or more away on the other side of the road.

"Ki!" Jessie called. She knew she risked the sniper's locating her by spotting the point her voice came from, but she took the chance because the ambusher had already shown that he was more likely to miss her than hit her with a long-range shot.

"I'm all right," Ki called in reply. Then he added, "You seem to be the target of those shots, not me."

"I'm sure I am," Jessie replied. "That first one was uncomfortably close."

"As long as it missed," Ki replied. ''Keep an eye on my horse, Jessie. I'm going scouting."

Knowing Ki's skill enabled him to move virtually unseen even in daylight, Jessie wasted no breath or time arguing. She kept her eyes in the direction his voice had come from and in a moment saw the suggestion of a flickering shadow in that area. The movement was so slight and vanished so quickly that only someone acquainted with Ki would know that he was moving toward the unseen gunman.

Like Jessie, Ki had not been able to mark the spot from which the sniper was shooting when the rifle's first shot shattered the evening silence. When the second shot was fired, he'd located the general area where the ambusher was concealed. Now, he moved silently and unseen, his body flattened to the ground. His black garb gave an onlooker the illusion that he was only a shadow caused by the approaching twilight.

As his eyes flickered across the terrain between himself and the area that he must reach, Ki was able to pick out the best route by which to approach. He did not go in a straight line, but in an arc that would allow him to approach his quarry from behind. He moved, his arms stretched in front of him. He propelled himself by bringing up one leg, then the other, and digging in his toes in order to push his body ahead.

Ki's progress was both swift and steady. He was almost close enough to his quarry to reach him with the sharp blade of one of the *shuriken* that were in the leather case strapped to his forearm. He heard the *thunk*ing of hoofbeats. Taking the risk of raising his head, he levered up to get a quick look at the approaching rider.

By now the evening had reached that point where in the high foothill range of northeastern Colorado the sunlight fades rapidly before it gives way to a brief dusk that quickly becomes darkness. The horseman approaching, like the sniper who had tried to cut down Jessie and Ki, was still too far away to be a certain target for a *shuriken.*

Kid did not get a clear look at the rider's face until the man reined in and dismounted. He turned toward Ki as he angled away from his horse. Ki recognized him instantly. The newcomer was Sir Albert Gray. Suddenly several things became clear.

Gray's departure from the ranch had not been the panic-stricken flight that Ki and Jessie had imagined it to be, but a carefully planned disappearance. Longarm had failed to find the cartel operative on the train in Denver because Gray had not been a passenger. The cartel boss had instead been traveling to some prearranged rendezvous with a force of gunmen who would carry out a full-scale attack on the ranch.

Even with the few facts of which Ki was certain, he was reasonably sure that Gray's orders must be to wipe out anyone who might interfere with the cartel's plan to gain control of the bulk of prairie in the Colorado and Wyoming Territories.

Ki's realization of Gray's motives led him to speed up his approach. The dusk was growing deeper minute by minute, and Ki lost no time in taking advantage of the fading light. He rolled now instead of crawled, which enabled him to cover the ground almost twice as fast. Within a very few moments, he could hear Gray talking to the sniper.

"And I told you not to use that rifle unless you were damned sure of hitting what you aimed at!" Gray said.

"I was sure, boss!" the man protested. "I had that Starbuck dame dead in my sights, but she wheeled around just when I triggered off my shot!"

Ki recognized the sniper's voice now. He'd heard it at the hole when the outlaws were holding him prisoner, but he could not put a name to the speaker. He edged forward carefully to get within throwing distance of the cartel boss and his hireling.

"All right," Gray said. "Whatever damage you've done to our plan can't be cured. But you're not doing any good out here now that the Starbuck woman and the Chink have gone to cover."

"Just give me one more crack at 'em!" the sniper said. "They can't stay outa sight forever, and I'll be damned sure to get at least one of 'em when they start for the ranch house."

For a moment Gray was silent. Then he said, "I guess you might get one of them even if it is getting dark."

"I just about guarantee it!" the sniper boasted.

"It'll be worth a lot of money to you if you do," Gray said. "If you can pick off the Starbuck woman or that damned Chink, I'll see that you get an extra cut."

"Now, that's the kind of talk I cotton to!" the outlaw said. "Don't worry, boss. I'll get one of 'em—maybe both if they don't move too fast."

"Stay here," Gray told him. "But remember what I told you to do. When our main bunch hits the house on the east, you get to this side of it as fast as you can. As soon as the boys on the far side have whoever's in the house pinned down, I'll come to the back door with Tobe and the three of us will break in and take them from behind."

"What about the hands in all them little houses back of the main house?" the sniper asked. "They're bound to come boiling out soon as the shooting starts."

"They won't get very far," Gray replied, his voice arrogantly confident. "Jenkins is seeing to that. He'll be ready with a shotgun to bottle the hands up in that lane between the corrals when they start for the main house."

Ki had continued his slow, silent advance while Gray was repeating his instructions to the sniper. Holding a *shuriken* in his hand, he was now within certain throwing range. He saw Gray start to walk back to his horse and wondered why Jessie did not shoot, but no report came from the knoll where she was concealed.

Gathering his knees beneath him and ready to spring up and loose the *shuriken* as soon as the cartel boss was outlined against the horse, Ki suddenly realized the opportunity that his knowledge of Gray's scheme offered. He did not move when Gray mounted, but waited until he'd ridden off. Then he advanced a few feet closer to the sniper.

He could see the man fairly clearly now. He was lying prone, his rifle shouldered and his head bent as he kept the weapon's sights on Jessie's position. Feeling over the ground, Ki ran his fingers silently in the soil until he found a stone. He pried it loose from its dirt bed and tossed it at the sniper. Ki's aim was good and the rock sailed true. It landed on the outlaw's back. The man leaped to his feet, swinging the muzzle of his rifle in Ki's direction. The surprise of the rock striking his back stripped away his caution.

Ki had his *shuriken* ready. The blade shimmered, a silver arc in the dimming twilight. Its twirling points slashed into the one vulnerable spot that was fully exposed, his jugular vein.

Dropping his rifle, the outlaw clawed at the blade with both hands. His spurting blood stained his fingers, and he could not stop the flow. His knees sagged and his hands fell away from his throat as he folded slowly to the ground and lay motionless.

Ki stood up now and called, "Jessie!"

"I'm here, Ki," she replied.

Seeing her get to her feet, Ki started toward her. He said, "Why didn't you shoot when you saw Gray? I expected you to fire any minute."

"I was afraid I'd spoil your plan," Jessie replied. "I saw Gray ride up, but didn't recognize him for a moment. About that time, I knew you must be closer to him than I was, even though I didn't know exactly where you were. I thought I might spoil whatever plan you might've made, and there was the danger that you might stand up between me and Gray as I shot."

"You showed your usual good judgment," Ki said. "And I've learned enough to spoil their ugly scheme. Let's get to the horses and hurry to the house, Jessie. We can talk on the way there."

As they rode toward the main house, Jessie asked, "Why didn't you take Gray with a *shuriken*, Ki? You must've been within easy range."

"I was close enough, but I let him go because while I was waiting for the right time to use my *shuriken* I overheard him going over his plans with the man who ambushed us."

"They're going to attack the ranch, aren't they? That's why Longarm couldn't find Gray on the train in Denver."

"Yes," Ki said. "And we've got a chance to kill two birds with one stone, the birds being the cartel and the outlaw gang from the hole. But we'll have to work fast."

"Then tell me your plan, Ki," Jessie said. "We'll be at the main house in about two more minutes. With that kind of opportunity, I'd hate to see anything go wrong."

•   •   •

Lights were shining through the half-drawn curtains of the first floor windows of the big stone house, but on the second floor the windows were all dark when the outlaws attacked. They swooped down from the line of low hills that rose just east of the building, and from her vantage point at one of the second floor windows, Jessie counted more than a dozen riders during the few moments it took them to reach the building.

Shots broke the evening hush and red spurts stabbed the gathering darkness as the attackers drew close to the house. There were a few tinkling crashes of broken glass when a slug here and there broke a window. Yells rose from the riders. Most of them were now zigzagging and firing at random. As yet no return fire had come from the house, and the attackers were yelling with joy at what they saw as a sure victory—with easy looting to follow.

"Give me three or four minutes," Ki told Jessie. "Tom and Pamela won't fire until you've let off your first shot, and I need just enough time to take care of Jenkins."

"He's still in the kitchen?" she asked.

"Yes—at least he was when I looked in there a minute ago," Ki replied. "But it's time now for him to do the job Gray gave him."

Since Jessie and Ki had reached the house only a few minutes earlier, Ki had watched the butler covertly. Jenkins had given him no indication that he knew of the coming attack. He'd paid no attention to them when they came in, but had carried out his routine duties as usual, moving between the kitchen and dining room in his preliminary preparations for dinner.

Now, Ki left the defense to Jessie and hurried downstairs. As he went through the swinging door between the dining room and kitchen, he glimpsed Jenkins stealing out the back door, a shotgun in his hand. Silently, Ki followed.

Lights showed now from the small houses of the hands

beyond the corrals and barn. Doors were opening. Ki had no difficulty following the butler with the lights silhouetting Jenkins' massive figure. The cartel raiders were closing in on the house, made bold by the lack of resistence. When Jessie's first shot cracked and Pamela and Tom began shooting, the riders were momentarily thrown into confusion.

Ki paid no attention to the firing. Jenkins was in the wide path that separated the twin corrals, walking steadily to meet the hands who were rushing toward the scene of the attack.

With a burst of speed, Ki caught up with Jenkins. The soft soles of his sandals made no sound on the packed earth, so the butler did not hear him approaching until Ki raised his voice in the shout that martial arts tradition demanded.

Startled by Ki's yell, Jenkins turned, raising his shotgun as he moved. Ki had known from the beginning that the weapon must be his first target. He whirled, starting a kick as his spinning body gained momentum and keeping his rising foot low enough to sweep the shotgun from Jenkins' hands and send it sailing over the corral fence to land in the center of the enclosure.

Jenkins took a short step toward Ki, bringing up his arms as he fell into a stance that marked him as a skilled boxer. Ki completed the turn forced on him by his kicking attack, and gaining still more bodily momentum, he lashed out with another kick. His heel pounded into Jenkins' belly. The big butler grunted as the force of the kick doubled him over, but he kept lurching forward, holding his arms wide and trying to grab Ki.

Ki evaded Jenkins' arms by dropping to his knees. While the butler was still moving ahead, unable to stop his arms from closing, Ki leaped to his feet. He folded his arms across his chest as he rose and brought them sweeping around, first the left hand and then the right, to smash Jenkins' larynx with one blow and crack his spine with the second. Like a poleaxed ox, the giant dropped to the ground and lay still.

Only two or three minutes had passed during the fight between Jenkins and Ki. The hands were in the corral now. They did not wait to saddle their ponies, but leaped on them and rode bareback, galloping out of the corral and toward the attacking outlaws. Their rifles began cracking before Ki reached the back door of the ranch house, and Ki felt safe in leaving to them the job of repelling the outlaws.

Opening the kitchen door just wide enough to allow him to slip inside, Ki entered the kitchen. Jessie was not there yet, and he started across the room to blow out the lamps that burned on each side of the stove. He saw as he reached the first lamp that it would be impossible to blow it out without lifting it from its bracket. Standing on his tiptoe, he reached up to extinguish it by turning down the wick.

At that moment he heard the knob of the back door rattle. Looking over his shoulder, he saw Gray framed in the open doorway. The cartel man had glimpsed Ki first and was already raising his revolver when Ki turned. Before Gray could bring up his gun, a shot barked from the door that led to the dining room. Gray's hand sagged from the weight of his heavy Webley pistol, and the bullet skidded along the tiles of the kitchen floor.

When Ki saw the cartel boss begin crumpling, he glanced at the inner door. Jessie stood there, her Colt still leveled. She fired again before Ki could move or speak, and when he turned away from the wall, the outlaw with Gray was toppling to fall across Gray's inert form.

"Are you all right, Ki?" she asked.

"Of course, but I didn't think I would be a minute ago."

"I'm sorry I was late," Jessie said.

"You got here in time, and that's what matters. Do the

men outside need some help?"

"No, they've killed all but three or four. They're chasing down the ones that're still left. From the way things look, the cartel's not going to have much strength in this part of the West for a while.

"We'll have to keep an eye on this part of the country, though," Ki warned her. "The cartel's like one of those snakes that keeps threshing around even after its head's been cut off."

"We'll have Don Carter close by," Jessie reminded him. "He'll get that land, now that the cartel's crippled. Don was with us on the Circle Star long enough to smell trouble before it gets too far along."

"Something else had just occurred to me, too," Ki said. His face was expressionless, but a hint of a smile flickered across his lips.

"What's that?"

"You'll have a very good reason now to stop in Denver. I'm sure you'll want to thank Longarm and explain why he didn't find the man you asked him to look for."

Jessie's face was as expressionless as Ki's as she nodded and said, "Of course, I will. I was just thinking about that myself."

Watch for

LONE STAR AND THE GULF PIRATES

forty-ninth novel in the exciting LONE STAR
series from Jove

coming in September!